THE DESPERATE DIARY
OF A COUNTRY HOUSEWIFE

Daisy Waugh is a journalist and travel writer. She has worked as an agony aunt and as a restaurant critic. She was a teacher at a girl's school in Northern Kenya and has also written a weekly column from Los Angeles about her attempts to become a Hollywood scriptwriter. Her previous novels include *The New You Survival Kit*, *Ten Steps to Happiness*, *Bed of Roses* and *Bordeaux Housewives*.

Daisy and her family live in London . . . for the moment.

D0807467

Two summers ago, Martha Mole and family moved from London to start a new life in the Country. It didn't go as smoothly as planned.

She kept the following diary. It should be noted, however, that there may have been times when her imagination got the better of her.

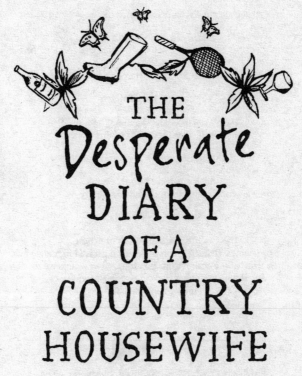

THE Desperate DIARY OF A COUNTRY HOUSEWIFE

A Cautionary Tale

HARPER

HarperCollins*Publishers*
77–85 Fulham Palace Road,
Hammersmith, London W6 8JB

www.harpercollins.co.uk

This paperback edition 2008
1

First published in Great Britain by HarperCollins*Publishers* 2007

Internal illustrations © Joy Gosney 2007

A catalogue record for this book
is available from the British Library

ISBN-13 978 0 00 726523 7

This novel is entirely a work of fiction.
The names, characters and incidents portrayed in it are
the work of the author's imagination. Any resemblance to
actual persons, living or dead, events or localities is
entirely coincidental.

Set in Giovanni Book by Andrew Ashton

Printed and bound in Great Britain by
Clays Ltd, St Ives plc

FOR MY HUSBAND

With many thanks to Lynne Drew, Carey Scott, Claire Bord, Stephanie Clark, Kelly Pike, John Witherow, Clare Alexander, Peter Conradi and anyone at HarperCollins or the *Sunday Times* who has been remotely involved (in a positive way) with any aspect of this project. Thanks to all the lovely estate agents. And thanks to my family.

OCTOBER 2007

About a year before our adventures began I dreamed of a house set in fields, with a moat round it. It was ramshackle and much too big, hidden away in a secret, sunny coomb that nobody but I knew about. I think it may have looked a little like a medieval castle, with tumbling ramparts and a drawbridge, and yet simultaneously like a large terraced house somewhere in Notting Hill Gate.

In any case, in my dream I knew it was the house we'd been searching for. Not only that, I knew that this beautiful dream house, though surrounded by rivers and fields, was also within walking distance of Hammersmith tube station. And it was for sale. And it was being snapped up — not by an annoying Russian oligarch, nor even by my brother-in-law, the amazingly successful banker. It was being snapped up by us. We — husband, the two children, myself, and a mysterious brown puppy calling itself Mabel — were trading it in for our ordinary terraced house in Shepherds Bush, with its views over three giant satellite dishes and a multi-storey car park, and we were going to live there, a life of carefree rural bliss, happily and wholesomely, for ever after. I remember waking up feeling exhilarated. And the feeling lasted, as I waded hither and thither through the usual Shepherds Bush knife victims and sundry litter, pretty much for the rest of the day.

The quest to find a place more satisfactory than Shepherds Bush to raise our young children continued as it had before. The husband and I had bored ourselves to sleep sometimes, discussing the options: Los Angeles? Sri Lanka? Sydney? New York? Ealing Common? ... Not all the suggestions were realistic of course, but because, like everyone else's, the value of our ordinary terraced house seemed to quadruple each fortnight, almost every option we threw in, however absurd, felt vaguely, distantly possible.

And there was always one thing we seemed to agree upon — that pretty much anywhere would be preferable to Shepherds Bush.

So we talked and we talked. And we talked and we talked.

And we talked.

And then one day, suddenly, the talking finished. We had made a decision.

I wonder now, with the benefit of the awful year and a half behind me, whether we were simply defeated by the sheer boredom of it. There came a point, perhaps, where neither of us could endure the conversation a moment longer.

... New Orleans? Kirkbymoorside? Malibu? Pitlochry? Nassau? Switzerland? Isle of Man? Barbados? King's Cross? Marylebone? Bordeaux? Lamu? Winchester? Westchester? Henley? Delhi? ...

The South West.

The following diary has been edited slightly — I've obscured a few names (or changed them) and for obvious reasons I've removed any give-away clues to our precise location. Otherwise it stands pretty much as I wrote it, a fairly accurate record of one very urban woman's foolhardy — idealistic — attempts to adapt to family life in the English countryside.

I'd seen the property programmes. I'd read the lifestyle magazines. I'd looked in awe — and guilt — at the happy, healthy faces of those young families who dared to leave the Big Smoke behind them. They always make it look so easy. Don't they.

The following should be looked upon as a cautionary tale.

May 21st 2005
Shepherd's Bush

We've found it. Finley and I have just got back from a day trip to Paradise, and the long, long search is over. At last.

This one may not have a moat around it, or any ramparts, and it's probably a four-hour drive from London. But it has the same magical, forgotten feeling as the house from the dream that I had, and when I saw it – when I turned the final corner of that winding path and looked up, and saw it properly for the first time – I swear it was so lovely it took my breath away.

The house is in the middle of a small village and just three miles up the road from a beautiful, old-fashioned market town. It perches alone, big and solid and perfectly symmetrical, on a hill so steep and so high above the village road that when you look up towards it all the proportions seem distorted. Actually it reminds me of an Addams Family cartoon: quite grand, in a way, though clearly dilapidated; with a stone porch, and in front of the porch a stone terrace, and in front of that a stone carved balustrade, drowning in jasmine and honeysuckle and ivy.

It has more bedrooms than we need, and more sitting rooms, and more cellars and underground vaults and cupboards and attics and cubbyholes than we'll ever know what to do with. But the children can build camps in them. That's the whole point. Or they can attach a rope ladder to the wall at the top of the back garden, and escape into the fields on the other side.

Not only that; it's only a few miles – almost bicycling distance – from the train station, which means, on a more practical note, that Fin can travel up and down to his office in Soho almost as easily as if he were taking the tube from Shepherds Bush. In fact everything about the house is so perfect, so romantic and so good for the trains, it seems quite peculiar that we can even afford it. Houses in this corner of the world are far from cheap. What with one thing and another – the beautiful, protected countryside, the trains that carry people so easily back and forth to Soho and the City – this is probably one of the most expensive corners of rustic paradise in England.

Maybe the fact that you can't get a car to the door might put a few people off. We both positively like that. It makes the place feel more secluded. In any case, with or without the access, this house could hardly be described as a cheapie and we are fully prepared to encumber ourselves with a monumental mortgage.

God knows, of all the options we've considered, the South West of England is hardly the most adventurous … but. But. But. But. It works. The schools are good. The house – I think I dreamed of. And in any case, whatever happens, however it turns out, we've been festering in London for far too long. It's about time we had an adventure.

We put our London house up for sale within the week, and made
an offer for the Dream House that afternoon. It was rejected out
of hand. So we upped the bid. They didn't even bother to respond.
Two days later we saw the house advertised in the Sunday Times.
So we sulked for a few days and then upped the bid again. And
again.

June 2005
Shepherds Bush

The horrible 'vendors'– him with his self-important beard;
her with her sour mouth and her chignon – have finally
accepted our offer. Bastards. Their obstinate refusal to sell
us the house for anything less than it's actually worth has
led me to develop a searing hatred for them both, and
especially for the woman – whose chignon, by the way,
isn't elegant, as she thinks it is, but actually quite embarrassing. Never mind, though. In my new country persona
I've definitely decided I'm going to try to stop being such a
bitch. I'm going to focus on people's positive sides. So.

On a more positive note, we've pretty much sold in
Shepherds Bush. It was all very quick and easy. Slightly
too quick, in fact. Unlike Beardie and the Chignon, we
didn't insist on getting the highest price. So now we're
about to exchange contracts, and we have to be out of

this house by the first week of July ... which leaves us homeless for about two months. Too long, really, to invite ourselves to stay with parents or friends. So we'll have to rent somewhere. Maybe we'll rent abroad, since the children are on holiday. Why not? I have the next novel due in before too long and I can write it wherever I like. In fact that's one of the reasons we can move out of London. And Fin will be away filming anyway.

In any case, if all goes according to plan the Dream House will be ours some time at the end of August.

2 a.m., July 10th
Shepherds Bush

Will I wind up wearing a chignon and having a mouth like an old cat's arse? Or will it be worse than that? Will I turn fat and mousey, and never get out of my anorak? Or will I hit the bottle and never get out of bed? Will my friends keep in touch with me? Will I keep in touch with them? Will Fin get a lover in London and never come home? Will I –

I've been lying here worrying for hours, thinking maybe we're making a terrible mistake, thinking maybe we'd be better off staying in London after all – and then I heard it, the old muffled smash, the panicky boot-shuffle, the ruffle-ruffle-*slam*: a series of sounds so familiar to Shepherds Bush night life I could probably recognise them from my sleep, integrate them seamlessly into any one of my dreams.

It is the musical sound of yet another car windscreen biting the dust. Not ours, though, on this occasion. It can't be, unfortunately, because we still haven't fixed ours from the week before last.

Maybe I should call the police?

Shall I call the police? Can I be bothered? It means getting out of bed, and then they probably won't even pick up the telephone ... Or if they do, they'll get here too late to do anything about it. And I'll have to give them my name and address and possibly even a cup of tea, and it'll wake up the entire house and the children will never go back to sleep and the whole thing will be a waste of time. I can't be bothered.

Maybe I should just knock on the window and give the little sods a jolt by shaking my fist at them? Or maybe I shouldn't. Not much to be gained from being a have-a-go hero in this dark corner of the woods. A couple of boys kicked through the front door of Number 35 last week, with the owners inside and screaming. I certainly wouldn't want to encourage that.

What shall I do then? Switch on the telly and pretend I can't hear them? Except the remote's broken. No, I think I'll just lie here until it goes quiet out there and then, er, put down the diary and go to sleep. Next time they come, maybe I'll call the police.

Except I won't, of course, because there won't be a next

time. We'll be gone. We'll have left it
all behind: street crime, parking
fines, Ken Livingstone, *London* …
We've had enough of it all.

I think we have.

At any rate I hope we have, because
most of our belongings are already in storage half way up
the M5. Finley, the two children and I – and the new
puppy (called Mabel, after the dream) – we're moving on.
To a new and fragrant life in the slow lane. We will be
joining that peculiar section of the human race that
doesn't get baity when queuing. Somehow. And there's
clearly not a single reason to be feeling nervous about it.

In any case the children and I – and Finley and his
mobile, intermittently – have a good long break in France
ahead of us, to mull the thing over.

It's a rough old life.

July 21st
France

Things have gone a bit crazy in London since we left.
According to my radio there's a suicide bomber hiding out
on our old street, and the whole area's been evacuated.
Nobody's dead. I don't think the bomb even went off. But

the terrorist is still very much at large. And in our street!

Should I call some of our old neighbours to commiserate, or would it seem like gloating? Don't know. Would dearly love to discover whose garden he's hiding in, though. Because if he leapt over the wall from the tube station, as they're saying he did, he must be on our side of the road, which means he might even be in our garden. Ex-garden, that is.

In any case, it's all very ... *exciting*'s the wrong word, of course. Shocking. *Shocking*. Poor old London. I suddenly feel a bit like a rat deserting a sinking ship. Awful. On the other hand it is slightly annoying, after ten years putting up with all those boring, unsolved low-level mini-crimes, to be missing out on the big one. Our old house might even be on the news.

Ripley and Dora found a drowned hedgehog in the swimming pool earlier this morning. Their obsession with all aspects of the ongoing – and apparently endless – embalming-and-burial ceremony is teetering on fetishistic, I think. Dora claims she's been studying the Egyptians at school but it's the first time she's mentioned it, and I don't know what R's excuse is. Last I saw, he had covered the wretched animal in yoghurt and very small lumps of Playdough; and Dora, in mystical monotone, was invoking 'voodoo and death spirits' over the body. Is that what people did to the Pharaohs? I think not. In any case I'm finding it faintly disturbing. Also wasteful of yoghurt and needlessly untidy. Perhaps this news from home might distract them a bit.

August 14th

Still in France. Lovely. Bad economics, perhaps. But we had to go somewhere. The Dream House is due to become officially ours exactly two days after we get back. We exchange and complete simultaneously. Which means – as Fin so wittily insists on pointing out – we could still duck out if we wanted to. We could still change our minds.

Except *we don't want to*. Everything's going to be wonderful.

Also, Hatty called this morning. Took a break from her very important job looking after other people's billions to tell me she had read somewhere, possibly in *Heat*, that Johnny Depp had just bought a small stately home in the same area as our Dream House. The article didn't say exactly where it was, but apparently JD and the wife, who I know is famous but can't remember her name, have been touring all the schools in what is about to be our local town. Which means they'll have done a tour of

Ripley and Dora's school. Which means – perhaps – that Ripley and Dora and the little Deppies could wind up being in the same classes together, which means they could wind up being friends! Which means *we* could be friends!

I picture us now: JD – and the wife – and all the other new friends we're going to make … I can see us relaxing on our beautiful terrace. The children are upstairs, snoozing. (Perhaps the little Deppies are upstairs with them, having a sleepover.) And we're drinking wine, we're talking films and novels, we're basking in the warmth of our outdoor heaters, watching the stars in the big, open sky and then maybe … God, I dunno. Perhaps Johnny produces a couple of grams of –

Dora, Ripley and I are going to bake cakes together, and pick apples together, and speak to each other in French. We're going to build bonfires and learn the names of wild flowers, and plant a Christmas tree so we can use the same one every year. We're going to learn to ride, and I might get some geese and a little Jersey cow, and every day after school we're going to climb up into the fields and the woods behind the house, and – yes – go *kite flying*. And we'll have picnics together, and read old-fashioned novels out loud to one another: *Swallows and Amazons*, for example. *Black Beauty*. *Treasure Island*. *Little Women*. Maybe, when they're older, even a bit of Dickens …

I've not been a perfect mother up until now. I've been chaotic and impatient and always in a hurry and usually hung-over and constantly preoccupied, if not by my work then by chatting to my friends on the blower. I hate cooking. I hate making angel get-ups out of cardboard. I never remember whose friend is coming to tea on what day, or when the term starts. I love it when the children watch DVDs. And I always forget to go to parents' evenings. *Mea culpa*. That's enough of that. They know I love them, I suppose.

In any case all that's going to change from now on. It is.

For example, I've ordered the sew-on nametags. There's something special about sew-on nametags, of course. They're a sort of 'From a good home' branding mark; possibly a 'My mother doesn't work' branding mark, too (but I mustn't be bitter). Either way, they shout of stable upbringings, balanced diets, selfless parenting and *time management at its best*. So I've ordered the nametags and if it kills me, I am going to sew them on. It will be the first step in what I fully intend to be a long and glorious transition from hassled, incompetent and very slightly selfish urban working mother to laid-back earth-mother-style Domestic Goddess. That's right.

I will still work, of course. But I'll do it when the children are asleep or at school. Or something. And after school the children will be free to play in the fields, and I won't sit on the sidelines muttering to myself over the newspapers. In fact I may even give up reading newspapers altogether. And the time that I save not reading them I shall now spend playing with the children because from now on – and this is a promise –

I am going to be a completely different human being.

September 1st

On the ferry home at last. Lots of fat, bored, hideous teenagers wandering around eating crisps and shouting. Is it possible that Ripley and Dora might one day turn into flabby, oral-fixated morons just like these? And if so, do I really want to be stranded with them, day after day, deep in the English countryside, while my husband travels up and down to Soho? Possibly not.

Ripley and Dora have gone to explore, by which they mean find the sweet shop. Fin's reading a film script. He has another one resting beneath it, ready for him to read after that. And it occurs to me I'm feeling more than a little bit irritable. Not surprisingly, perhaps. We're due to exchange and complete on the new house the day after tomorrow, and we've neither of us set eyes on it since May.

Thousands of people do what we're doing. Families move out of London every day, and they all claim to be very happy about it. They can't *all* be lying. Can they? It's going to be wonderful. It's going to be better than wonderful.

I wonder if Johnny Depp plays tennis?

Monday September 3rd

Filthy weather. Bloody England.

The estate agent made it clear he didn't want us to visit the house this morning. He tried hard to sound too busy to fit us in, but it was obvious he had nothing else to do. I got the distinct impression he was suppressing a yawn for the entire conversation.

So we left the children with Finley's parents and drove over. Looking at the map, we thought it would take only about forty-five minutes but – fresh to this bucolic existence as we are – we hadn't fully taken into our calculations the tractor factor.

In any case the journey took over two hours, just as Finley's father had always warned us it would. He says the journey could never really take less than two hours because if there aren't tractors blocking the way there'll be a couple of oldies, killing a little of their excess time by driving somewhere unnecessary as slowly as mechanically possible, specifically to annoy the younger people who are running late in the long line of cars behind them. Well, no, he didn't say that exactly. In fact he didn't say it at all. He just said people drove slower in the country, and to be careful of speed cameras.

Goodness, though, there do seem to be an awful lot of

elderly persons in this corner of the countryside. Which isn't necessarily a bad thing, of course. Of course, of course. Oldies have to live somewhere, don't they? And so on.

The last time we saw the Dream House was on a beautiful sunny day back in May. The grass had been freshly cut and there was honeysuckle growing in vast, sweet-smelling clumps all over the terrace balustrade. It was breathtakingly pretty. It was beautiful.

This morning the honeysuckle was long gone. The sky was low and black, and it was raining. Not only that, the garden clearly hadn't been touched since the day we last came to see it, nearly four months ago.

We found Richard the estate agent waiting for us, yawning and stretching, managing to look simultaneously self-righteous and half asleep. We trampled up the path towards him, apologising for the tractors and the old people and the resulting need to reschedule (we had called to postpone the meeting). It all seemed to be going down OK– in fact he almost cracked a smile – but then, just as Fin and I climbed the final step to the front porch, I accidentally trod on a slug.

It was the size of a small serving spoon, I think; possibly even larger. And I screamed. I couldn't help it. I was only wearing thin canvas trainers, and so my foot had clearly experienced each stage of the slug's final moment: the pathetic, rubbery resistance, the deathly squelch … It was not good. So I screamed. And the other thing I did, unfortunately, was I shouted '*Fuck!*' Once again, I couldn't help it. Sometimes these words have to come out.

Richard the estate agent looked at me as if I'd just brought out a machete and threatened to cut off his cock. Wish I had, actually. Might have livened him up a bit. In any case I apologised profusely, of course. But some people just won't accept apologies, will they? He could hardly bring himself to look at me after that. Sulkily, he turned back to the front door, slid the key into the lock – and then paused.

'The office just called, by the way,' he said. He had to shout over the sound of rain gushing from the broken gutter above our heads. 'You'll be delighted to hear we're ahead of schedule. You and the vendors exchanged and completed contracts about half an hour ago.'

'Ooh sugar!' I chortled (trying to suck up, obviously, after the swearing débâcle. Richard the estate agent would be getting no more fucks from me). 'Don't suppose we can sidle out of it now, then, can we?'

'Not easily, no,' he said drearily, looking only at Fin.

Fin said 'Fantastic!' or something similarly delightful. I could see Richard's sullen shoulders slowly relaxing. Once again he very nearly smiled.

Fantastic Fin – always says the right thing in the right way to the right person, and wherever he goes he always leaves a trail of slowly relaxing shoulders behind him. But sometimes (I happen to know) he's being Fantastic on autopilot. He's actually not paying the slightest bit of attention to all the Fantastic words which are bubbling so agreeably out of his cakehole. Sometimes, for example, he's exchanging text messages with a film financier in Canary Wharf at the same time.

It doesn't matter, anyway. It's too late now. And the fact is I wasn't texting financiers at the time, and it didn't occur to me either – or not until just now (back at Fin's parents and after a long bath) – but I now think Richard the estate agent was probably lying when he said the house was already ours. We'd not been due to exchange and complete until the day's end, or so I had understood. And frankly, what with the rain and the broken gutter and the outrageously neglected garden, the house wasn't exactly looking …

Well it's still beautiful and everything, and big – and it's going to be lovely. I'm sure it's *going* to be lovely. But this morning it wasn't really looking its best. It was looking pretty awful. In fact there was a moment, as we stood on that leaking porch, and I still had bits of giant slug attached to my foot, when all I really wanted to do was run.

The feeling didn't last. Of course. Of course not. In any case the house is ours now, for certain. Gordon Brown has taken his monumental Stamp Tax. He has already tossed it into his big, black hole, never to be seen again.

And the house is ours. There can be no turning back.

September
Paradise

We've been in Paradise ten full days already and the sun has shone for every one of them. The sun is shining now. It's beaming down on us, and there are no slugs anywhere to be seen. Dora and Ripley are outside, and I can hear their squeals of laughter. Both seem to be very happy at their new school. Their new classmates are sweet and welcoming, and noticeably more innocent and less bratty than the little Londoners we left behind.

Ditto the mothers, actually.

Not one of whom, incidentally, seems to work. Their husbands, like Finley, commute back and forth to the capital, and they stay at home, just being mothers, and being really nice. Oh dear.

I've noticed they don't like it when I swear.

Fin is in London again, and plans to be all week. But I've just ordered the box set for Series 5 of *The West Wing*, and I still have three episodes of Series 4 to go, so I won't miss him … In my next life I plan to be a press secretary at the White House, with no children, sadly, but lots of clever colleagues and lots of Armani suits. In the meantime, all is good in Paradise. Tomorrow, after school,

Ripley, Dora and I are going to pick blackberries in the fields behind the house. For the first time ever, I think, I begin to feel almost smug about my mothering abilities, and the children's upbringing. It's all so wonderfully wholesome it makes my eyes water.

I just wonder why we didn't move down here years ago.

September 20th

The children's nametags arrived! Unfortunately I've got to do a book plug/radio interview all the way over in Plymouth this evening – assuming, that is, that Fin arrives back from London in time to babysit. Desperately need to get hold of a regular babysitter from somewhere – but where? I've asked numerous mothers, but they all seem to use the same person. Or there's one other girl somebody suggested, but she lives twenty-five miles away.

Any case, I will sew on the nametags tomorrow. Failing that will *definitely* do them over the weekend.

September 23rd

Fin's train was delayed, so I had to cancel the radio interview. *Shame*, as I said to Fin. Among numerous other things. But it made me stir my stumps on the babysitting front, and I think I've found someone at last. She's only slightly younger than I am and she has a couple of children, though she was a bit vague as to their whereabouts. I think maybe they live part time with the father. She has a disconcertingly soft voice so I can never hear a word she says. Also, she is strangely lifeless. Almost slug-like, in fact. Without being rude. Doesn't seem to react at ordinary speeds – or at all, really, to anything anyone says.

But I'm sure she's fine. Got her name off a card in the launderette and she showed me a couple of references. Funnily enough she looks incredibly familiar. I'm convinced I've met her before somewhere, but she denies it.

Not that we have much call for a babysitter at the moment. Or, to be honest, any call at all. But the Plymouth thing was annoying. I'd been looking forward to a few bright lights and so on. A bit of flattery. In any case, it's reassuring to know that we could now call on someone if, by some happy chance, Finley and I had the extraordinary good fortune ever to be invited anywhere again.

Every time I turn the corner and look up at the house I feel my heart lift. Because it's beautiful. And because the children are happy here. And because we have finally, at long last, escaped from London.

We had planned to wait and get all the refurbishment work done before we invited friends down to stay with us, but now that we're more or less settled I can't really see the point. Apart from the fact that we seem incapable of finding any builders, the house is perfectly comfortable as it is. It may be a bit short on furniture, but who cares? We've got a big sofa. And a telly. I'm going to buy a couple of extra beds and some sleeping bags and persuade Hatty (and family) to come and stay as soon as possible. I miss her. I miss all my friends. It's the only serious blot on an otherwise blemishless landscape.

October 10th

Bit of a culture shock at the weekend. Maybe it doesn't signify anything, but I can't stop thinking about it. The Mothers had told me about a stables which they all swore was the single riding school in the area worth using. So. The children have been desperate to take up riding. I rang the place up. And a woman at the other end advised me, with a certain amount of relish, that beginners' lessons were 100 per cent booked up, now and for the entire foreseeable future. She said that, for £10 per name, children could be put on to a waiting list. I complained, but it didn't move her much.

She softened a little, though, once I'd given my credit card details, and suggested it might be worthwhile just turning up one weekend and waiting around, on the off chance of a late cancellation. So – Finley was away. That's what we did on Saturday.

Horrible! It felt like we were walking into a Barbie Doll theme park. The yard was so tidy it ought to have had a pink plastic logo swinging over the front gate. Also it was teeming with lady-clones, all of them sporting the same tasteful blonde highlights and clean, green, calf-flattering Wellington boots. There must have been fifteen four-wheel drives in the car park and fifteen super-mummies milling around, fixating on the buckles of their children's safety hats. I recognised a handful of the women from school, of course. The question is, though, *Where did all the others come from?* I had no idea there were so many in the area. And I'm not sure whether to be depressed or very depressed by the discovery. What the hell's going on?

In any case, the children and I hung around for about an hour, patting ponies and being pretty much ignored, until finally a lovely, rosy-cheeked teenager came over to talk to us. There had been no last-minute cancellations, she said, but she offered, out of kindness, to put the children on top of an old donkey and lead them round the yard a couple of times.

Ripley and Dora were having the time of their lives, squeezed together on top of the old donkey, giggling blissfully as it slowly plodded along. They've never ridden before. They were thrilled. Rosy Cheeks was giving them a little impromptu lesson, and the love was flowing between all of us, Rosy Cheeks, Ripley and Dora, the donkey, even me.

But then suddenly, careering out of nowhere, there came a very thin, very angry woman. She was screaming at us because Ripley and Dora, approximately 3 feet off the ground, travelling at significantly less than 1 mile per hour, and with an adult ready to catch them on either side, had not been strapped into safety helmets.

Rosy Cheeks turned purple and looked like she was about to cry. I tried to point out how entirely undangerous the situation was for all concerned, and that I was positively grateful that my children had been allowed to go bare-headed. 'It's nice to feel some wind in the hair occasionally,' I said. Which was perhaps a little provocative. Or maybe not. In any case, at that point the Pipecleaner turned her great ire solely onto me. This wasn't about danger, she sneered. Danger had nothing to do with anything. It was about liability. 'And you ... *people* ... always sue.'

Do we? Do I?

Anyway Ripley and Dora were forced to dismount, which they did with great stoicism and dignity, I thought. Ripley gave the old bag his most baleful glare, but she didn't appear to notice. And we left the stable yard under a great cloud of disgrace. We headed back to our car, past all the super-mummies standing white-knuckled with fear while their precious offspring, in full body armour, plodded clockwise round the schooling ring.

They stared at us as we scuttled by – at my hatless children in pity, I think, and at Rosy Cheeks and me as if we were murderers.

Dora giggled. 'I don't think she liked us *at all*,' she said.

I opened up the sun roof as we drove away. I think I must have been doing it to bait, because I knew the children would immediately poke their heads out of the top.

I ordered them to sit down. But I didn't really mean it, and the children could tell. They rolled back their hatless heads and roared with laughter.

Ripley and Dora now say they want to go riding again, which is good in a way, I suppose, but also slightly depressing. Unless, of course, I can ferret out an alternative riding school, where the super-mummies and their fun-sucking safety obsessions haven't yet cast a pall.

Sunday night, October 21st

Hatty, Damian and the Psycho Kids just left. Thought I'd feel a bit wistful, seeing them head off back to the Old Smoke. But no. Far from it. Truth be told I was quite relieved to see the back of them. It's been a long weekend.

Poor Hatt. She and Damian aren't exactly seeing eye to eye at the moment. In fact, now I think of it, I'm not sure they even glanced at one another for the entire weekend. And Damian's a pretentious little git. (Even Fin agrees, and I can't usually get Fin to be horrible about anyone.) But there's no denying he's handsome. Now that Hatty can't even bring herself to look at him, I don't see how she can draw any pleasure from their partnership at all.

Damian writes screenplays for a living. Rather, he writes screenplays. He does about two hours' work a day, according to Hatt, and never, in all the time she's known him, earned a single penny from it – or from anything else, either. He spends most of his energy whining about President Bush, and then, when he's drunk a bit more (which he usually has), whining about the creative strain imposed on him by always having to scrounge off Hatty. Hedge Fund Hatt. She earns a fortune, it has to be said. But still.

So Damian doesn't really work, and he doesn't help much, either. He sat tight on that bony little arse of his the entire weekend. Didn't lift a buttock. Didn't clear a coffee cup. He barely spoke at lunch or dinner, and even in between times he didn't move from the kitchen table. He just sat there silently, occasionally clicking his tongue over the right-wing bias of the newspapers and calling for cups of tea.

It occurs to me suddenly that he may be suffering from depression. People often get fixated with current affairs when they're depressed. Or maybe it's the other way round. In any case, poor guy, I'm sure he didn't used to be quite so dismal. In fact, when he first came on the scene, and he was still full of ambition and hope and spunk and all, I have a fuzzy memory of his occasionally even being quite attractive.

As for the three children ('the Psycho Kids', as Dora calls them), I'm not sure what their excuse is. They have a nanny with more qualifications than a neurosurgeon during the week, and an adoring mother who dedicates herself to their every need at the weekends – and, truthfully, they're awful. They refuse to eat anything except bread and ketchup; they won't address a word to anyone but Hatt;

and they never go to bloody bed. On Saturday afternoon Hatty and I took them for a walk by the stream, and Lucia (aged 8) got her boot stuck in a puddle. For some inexplicable reason it sent her into a blood-curdling tantrum, the like of which I have never witnessed. I would have left her there, frankly. We were only a couple of hundred yards from home. But Hatty, who deals with tens of millions of pounds every day, or probably does, and is without doubt the most effective human being I know (as well as being my best friend), was almost in tears about it. Anyone would have thought the girl had trodden on a landmine, not in a puddle. In the end Lucia managed to make life so unpleasant for everyone we all had to turn round and go home.

...Hard not to feel a bit conceited about Ripley and Dora by comparison. All those years of slapdash, bad-tempered parenting and intermittent bargain-basement childcare seem to have done them the world of good.

So. That was our first attempt at weekend entertaining. I discover it's not quite so easy. Partly, I suppose, because we haven't really unpacked yet. But mostly because the whole process takes a hell of a lot more work than I'd realised. It's nobody's fault – certainly not Fin's, who more than pulled his weight – but I feel like I've been skivvying pretty much solidly since they arrived on Friday night. We spent £200 on food and slightly more on alcohol, I'm exhausted, and not even specially convinced anyone had a very nice time.

Other news ...

Hatty's been muttering for ages about raising funds to put one of Damian's unwanted screenplays into production, and I never really took her seriously. But I forgot: Hatty isn't like other people. One way or another she's now pulled together £50,000. She says she's raised it through her work connections, but I have a feeling she's saying that to protect Damian's feelings. I think she's raised it from her own bank account. In any case, it's enough to get the script for his five-minute short, called *Goodbye Jesus*, turned into screen reality, and with Hatty at the helm it looks like it might really get made.

Not only that, it turns out that Hatty's sister went to school with somebody who claims to be the best friend of the great Paul Bettany, and Hatty seems convinced that on the strength of that – let's face it – pretty feeble connection, Paul Bettany is going to play the lead part in *Goodbye Jesus*, and for free! Under normal circumstances I'd laugh, but knowing Hatty she'll probably pull it off.

Anyway she's been asking Finley for advice about film-making all weekend, which – I can't help noticing – he's been more than happy to provide. Now she's asked him over for dinner next week, in London. 'You don't mind, do you?' she said to me, and she was grinning. It was meant to be rhetorical. A joke. Of course.

'Mind? *Moi?*' I cried, laughing uproariously.

But I do mind, actually.

Two months away from London, and already I'm turning into a neurotic, jealous *hausfrau*. Too much time surrounded by fields, I suppose. Too much time to think. Hatt's my oldest friend, for Heaven's sake.

Seriously. How pathetic is that?

November 2nd

Fin got into London an hour late this morning because the earlier train was cancelled. He's already called me twice to complain about it. But what am I supposed to do?

He said it meant he was forced to miss a very important meeting, but – as I so hilariously pointed out to him – he has at least thirty very important meetings every day. Can it really matter if he misses one of them? I was being funny. I think. On second thoughts maybe I was just trying to annoy him. Any case, he didn't laugh, and now I need to ask him something about scaffolders because a gust of wind just knocked a massive chunk of lead guttering loose and it's swinging across the front of the house. I keep calling but he's refusing to pick up his telephone. Either that, of course, or he can't pick it up because he's in a meeting.

Wish I had a few meetings to go to.

November 7th

Got a hot date with a new friend called Rachel White. She is the ex-sister-in-law of my London accountant and she and her new husband, who is also an accountant, have invited us over to dinner on the Saturday evening after the Saturday evening after next. Fin's in New York at the moment, so I haven't confirmed it with him, but if he's not around I can just go by myself. I accepted for both of us in any case.

Our children go to the same school, though they're in different years, and I suppose my accountant must have mentioned something to her because she came over while I was lingering at the school gate, friendless and hopeful as ever, and very kindly introduced herself.

She was wearing tweed trousers with sensible brown slip-on shoes underneath, and a burgundy fleece with some sort of financial institution's logo sewn on above the left knocker. She has mousy grey hair, cut astonishingly badly, and a broad, ruddy, friendly, well-meaning face.

Christ. It's hardly Johnny Depp, is it? But we've got to start somewhere.

Talking of Johnny Depp, Clare Gower (of the school gate: her son, Joshie, is in the same class as Ripley; plus she has another, called Tanya, in the year above Dora) says she thinks she saw him in Waitrose on Tuesday! She's not sure it was him, though. In fact, on closer questioning it became pretty clear that she didn't really know who Johnny Depp was, nor had the faintest idea what he looked like. Nor much idea of anything else, either, come to that. Nevertheless, she said, and I quote:

'I wouldn't say I was absolutely certain, of course – wait a minute, Joshie, Mummy's talking. But, he certainly looked familiar, and if it wasn't Mr Deppy then it was the other chappie. The fellow in Batman. I mean Spiderman. Oh shoot … What's he called, Joshie, can you remember? That nice actor-man Mummy saw in Waitrose on Tuesday. Joshie's like a little fact machine, aren't you, Joshie? He's Mummy's little brainbox … Oh goodness, what's the fellow called? Leonardo Something. Leonardo Thingamajig.'

Clare Gower has invited me to a coffee morning next week, and I am happy to say that I have accepted.

R's lost his school jersey. Must do the nametags before anything else goes missing.

November 8th

Well whatdderyaknow? Just got off the blower with Hattie, who'd just got off the blower with Paul Bettany, who's apparently in London and 'at a loose end' for three days next week. He says that if she and Damian can pull the rest of the cast and crew together in time – and they will, or rather Hatty will – he's agreed to play the lead in her film. For free.

She says he's lovely, and I'm sure he is. I told her I'd seen him perform once, before he was famous, in a play at the Bush Theatre. He was brilliant, I said, and I would have been happy to expound a little, or even a lot. But she wasn't that interested. In any case she was in a rush. She mentioned that Finley was being incredibly helpful: that she'd been calling him up about twenty times a day the last couple of weeks – which is news to me – and that apparently, out of the kindness of his heart, he's given her the name of a young producer and some hot new director and a whole bunch of other people to help bring the project together. *Fantastic*. As Fin would say. God, he's so delightful.

Anyway, Hatty's leaving Damian in London to cast the leading girl, and she's taking time off work and flying out to Los Angeles tomorrow to meet up with Bettany. She giggled when I asked what she was going to talk to him about. She said she hadn't the foggiest. 'I'm really just going there to see if I can buy him dinner,' she said. 'And to *thank* him.' Ho-hum. Lucky thing.

Fin's in LA at the moment, of course. I have to admit I toyed with the idea of not mentioning that fact to Hatty. Not sure why. Well. Yes I am. In any case, I did tell her. And she already knew it. She'd just been speaking to him. In fact he'd advised her to check in to the same hotel. 'If I can't get Paul Bettany to have dinner with me which I probably can't ...'

'He's got a very beautiful wife, by the way,' I said sourly.

'Exactly. Which is why Fin and I are almost certainly going to meet up for dinner tomorrow night. He says he'll take me to the Ivy to cheer me up.'

Tuesday November 20th

Fin's just called to ask where he should buy a new sofabed. He says the one he has in his office is too lumpy, and given how many nights he's spending in London at the moment ('with the trains as they are') he wants to invest in a new one. He says he won't be coming down to Paradise before Friday again this week.

I decided not to kick up a fuss, mostly because, as Fin cleverly reminded me only this morning, it was my idea to move out to Paradise in the first place.

Doesn't matter, anyway. Got loads of telly to watch. Plus at some point I seriously ought to do some work. I'm so behind with the novel now it makes me feel sick whenever I think about it. Plus I've got an article to write about white wedding dresses (Yes or No?) and, though I distinctly remember injecting enormous amounts of passion into the discussion when the piece was commissioned, I've forgotten whether said passion was in favour or against, and since it's now almost two weeks overdue I'm hesitant to ring up and check. Also, much more excitingly, I have a cunning plan to write a newspaper column all about my strangely adventureless life out here in the sticks. Why not? I'd enjoy it, even if no one else did. It would almost be like having someone to talk to.

Truth is, though, I've slightly lost track of my laptop. This has never happened before. In London I used to write on it every weekday, like a normal person with a job to do. Plus I couldn't survive twenty minutes without checking my e-mail. In fact I virtually slept with the laptop under my pillow. Now I'm not even sure how many days ago it was that I last saw it. So what the hell's going on?

Might this be a first indication of a new unhurried, unworried persona emerging from my desiccated urban shell? I sincerely hope not, actually. Apart from the rest of it (and I'll need to make a real effort with the journalism if I'm to keep myself from being buried alive down here) there's the next novel to be delivered in three and a half months, and pretty much everything I've written so far looked like complete drivel, last time I read back. I think I'm going to have to start again.

Thursday November 22nd

Computer still not turned up. Ditto the nametags. Where did I put them? Ripley tells me he's lost his blazer, which I bought new for some incredibly stupid reason, also about forty-five sizes too large, so that it was virtually unwearable anyway. I wrote his name in biro on the label while I was waiting for the bloody nametags to arrive, but now he tells me the label was 'a bit itchy' and he cut it out.

£60 down the shit-hole, then.

I wonder if there's an agency somewhere that will sew people's nametags in for them? There must be. If I could find my wretched laptop I might be able to find out.

Monday November 26th

It occurs to me that I haven't laid eyes on my computer since that peculiar carpenter came round to measure up for bookcases over a week ago. I think he may have snuck it out with him when he left. Which explains a lot, actually. At the time he certainly had me fooled. I even felt a little sorry for him. Now, of course, I'm beginning to wonder if he was actually a carpenter at all.

He spent hours measuring up; literally *hours*, and then at the end, while he was still blowing gently over a stone-cold cup of tea, I asked him, not unreasonably I thought, how long he thought he might need to build the things. And he looked astonished. He looked quite put out. Five minutes passed with him carefully adjusting the position of his mug on the kitchen table, scratching on his fleabites and so on …

Until finally, very, very slowly, he said: 'Fact ezzz, Madam [*Madam*!] I can't say … Not in so many werrds … I wud if I cud, believe me … Much as I'd love if I cud, see … As the saying goes, *How long is a piece of string?*'

And that was it. Beyond that, however many times I asked, whichever way I phrased the question, he simply refused to be drawn.

I got his name off a card at the launderette, but that's hardly a solid endorsement, is it? If my laptop doesn't turn up soon I think I'm going to call the police.

Friday November 30th

Called the police. Funny. Ten years in Shepherds Bush and I never bothered to contact them once. Three months down here in Paradise and I've already got the number for the local station on speed dial. What does that say? Not at all sure, yet. But it must say something, mustn't it?

I had already explained how I wrote novels and magazine articles and so on, and about Ripley and Dora and the new dog called Mabel, and the move down from London. I'd explained that my husband was originally from Quebec but that he didn't really speak much French any more. I think I told him about my 2.1 in history, my antipathy to the London Olympics, and about my recently deceased great aunt who was allergic to oysters. So I was on the very point of handing over the carpenter's name and telephone number – when I spotted my precious laptop, nestling happily beneath a large dictionary on my, er, desk.

Luckily, I managed to get the policeman off the telephone without his suspecting anything. He's suggested I go down to the station to make an official statement. Which obviously I can't now, can I?

Shame.

Never mind. Tonight I have the mysteriously non-responsive and familiar-looking babysitter coming round. I'm going to dinner with Rachel White and her husband the accountant and, truth be told, I can't wait. I've not been out for so long now I don't think I've looked forward to an evening so much in years.

Unfortunately Fin's not going to be able to make it. He just called. One of his financiers pulled out this morning and the film is on the point of total collapse. So. He has meetings to go to. I hope Rachel doesn't mind. It's not his fault. There's really not much he can do about it, anyway. And she seems very nice. I'm sure she'll understand.

!!!!! She CANCELLED me! She bloody *CANCELLED* me!

I saw her at the school gate so over I scuttled, all smiley and super. I should have realised that things weren't going to be simple from the start, because I opened with a friendly-but-casual 'Hello, Rachel! Still on for tonight?'

And she definitely looked offended. 'Goodness, I should hope so,' she said.

I ploughed on in any case, friendly-but-casual as before.

'... He's so sorry,' I said. 'He was looking forward to this evening so much, but he's stuck in these awful meetings the whole night, and it was a choice, really: make the dinner party or save the film! So I'm afraid you're going to have to make do with just me!'

She shook her head, and I could tell before she spoke, by the shape her lips were making, that I'd got it wrong. I'd got everything completely wrong.

'Oh, what a *shame*!' she cried, almost as if I'd told her I had to amputate the leg. 'Oh, goodness, what a *shame*. Oh, that's such a *disappointment*!' The skin around her nostrils went red, and I realised with a chill that she wasn't looking at me any more.

I said, 'Rachel, he's so sorry. And so am I. But still *I'm* so looking forward –'

She said, 'Don't be silly. There's no way we're dragging you out in the middle of the night on your own. Certainly not.'

'But –'

'No. We wouldn't think of it. We wouldn't dream of asking such a thing.'

'But –'

'No.'

'But, please –'

But, no.

No.

And that was it. She said she'd make another date 'when Finley's schedule is a bit clearer', and she suggested we meet for 'a coffee' one day next week.

December 14th

Fin went to the screening of Hatty and Damian's short film last night. He said it was very, very good. Dying to see it.

I sent them a bunch of flowers for luck. Wonder if they arrived in time? Any case I'd better take the dog out. She's making funny coughing noises, and all the chocolate biscuits have gone missing. Got a feeling she's about to be sick.

December 15th

Half the builders I telephone don't even bother to return my telephone calls. The rest make appointments, and then never turn up. Can't quite work out what I'm doing wrong.

Fin, needless to say, has had a little more success. Somebody in London gave him the name of an Irish woman called Megan, who apparently once did some work for one of the Rolling Stones and who consequently (he'd been warned) presented herself very much as a Builder to the Stars.

He contacted her last Friday evening, and she hopped onto her broomstick there and then, arriving at our front door, hunchback and shoulders fully relaxed, dyed black hair perfectly coiffed and stout little body positively dripping in eighties-style jewellery, within an hour of his making the telephone call. How does he do it?

Sadly, however, we had to reject her. Or maybe she sadly rejected us. It was pretty clear from the beginning that we were singing from different hymn sheets.

'I can tell you're a woman with discerning taste,' she muttered to me, leaning her broomstick against the porch and shimmying into our untouched, half-lit, empty hallway. I felt quite aglow for a moment – until I looked up and down and around and about and realised she had absolutely nothing, at that early stage, upon which to base the observation.

Anyway. She took the briefest of glances round our bomb-site of a house and then, suddenly, looked at her watch and announced she had to leave. She couldn't possibly discuss budgets or plans with us, she said, until we had inspected the property she and 'her boys' were currently working on in a village about twenty miles away.

We went to look at it the next morning. A Saturday. It was a house belonging to a couple of art dealers from Seattle, neither of whom was present. Nevertheless I think she was quite put out that we tipped up with the children. It's possible she was quite put out that we tipped up at all.

The tour, which was made unnecessarily stressful by her rampant irritation with our fairly well-behaved children, seemed to go on forever. Fin and I were forced to admire every tap, every door handle, every eco-friendly window fastener in the building. And it wasn't easy. Somehow, and clearly at unimaginable expense, Megan and her team of boys had transformed what was once, presumably, a perfectly pretty village cottage into something that looked more like an industrial greenhouse.

At some point (about an hour in) she was distracted from her boasting by an improperly fitted cupboard latch, and we managed to slip away. She found us a couple of minutes later – Fin, me and the children – sardine-packed into what was meant to be her *pièce de résistance*: an aluminium, bean-shaped lavatory capsule, cleverly suspended above what would one day be a dining room. We were giggling quite a lot, testing out the motion-sensitive toilet flush. Or the children were. Or, no. We all were, in fact.

I think it dawned on Megan about then that we were completely out of our depth. The art dealers from Seattle were spending on a single, motion-sensitive lavatory pod about three times what we had to spend on our entire house.

Nevertheless, at the end of the tour we hugged each other passionately. We reconfirmed our various e-mails and telephone numbers and swore we'd speak again before the weekend was out, just to confirm budgets and dates and so on. That was over a week ago now. Obviously we've made no attempt to contact each other since.

And I never even asked her about Johnny Depp. As the West Country's designated Builder to the Stars she ought to know if there's any truth behind the rumours. I wish I could say I forgot to ask her, but the fact is she's slightly scary, and I didn't quite dare.

The good news is I now have another builder up my sleeve. He's called Darrell and he's coming round this evening. I saw his card pinned up in the village Co-op (as opposed to the launderette, where clearly the calibre of cards isn't up to scratch) and he sounds lovely. Quite sexy, actually. He says he's built hundreds of kitchens before. Not only that, he's available to start on ours immediately.

December 15th again

Bit drunk. Darrell has just left.

Darrell. *Darrell.* **Darrell.** Is about 6 foot 3 and outrageously good looking. Also he has amazingly long eyelashes. Also he's outrageously good looking. He's unbelievably good looking. Also – very sexy. He has a very sexy laugh. He stayed for two beers. Which he drink from the bottles. I think I knocked back five glass of wine, which I may have glugged a bit too quickly. Anyway, Darrell says he can start the kitchen on Monday. Christ. Things are looking up.

Also Dora says she left her swim kit somewhere. I called up, but nobody knews shag all about anything downethere.

Nametags tomorrow. Nametags nametags nametags nametags nametags namtags namtags namtagnametag-gssnamteags

Goodnight xxxxxxxxxxxxxx

December 17th

The prospect of the children's Christmas holidays, looming ever closer, has finally spurred me to get down to work. Written and filed the wedding piece, to resounding silence; which, I've decided, is a good sign. Also been asked to write a piece about my attitude to Advent calendars. Do I have one? I think not. Never mind. Most importantly, the Novel's finally moving along OK and I've even managed to write the first of my dummy country columns. I'm going to offer it around to newspapers next week. See if anyone bites.

Sooperdooper.

Wonder if Darrell and Co. want a cup of tea?

We've decided we're going to spend Christmas in Andalusia after all. Dad's still a bit ropey, but Sarah's pretty much adamant she wants us to come out and try to cheer him up a bit. I've told her we'll stay at the B&B in the village and she put on a very good show of saying no, but I think she was relieved when I insisted.

It means the great Christmas tree tradition (planting/replanting, etc.) will have to be postponed until next year. I've slightly gone off the idea anyway. Too many slugs. In any case, truth be told, I'm looking forward to a bit of sun.

Fin's in London again. Has been all week. I don't think I'll bother to mention my anonymous column to him, even if I sell it. It may inhibit what I want to write about him at a later date.

COUNTRY MOLE

Sunday Times

January

We did it. We made the break. We sold the place in Shepherds Bush and left the Big Smoke behind us. It took us years to make the decision, months to organise the move, but we escaped, finally, on July 4th 2005.

Seventeen days later one Hussein Osman (a.k.a. the Shepherds Bush Bomber) used our ex-neighbour's garden to hide out from the police, and our street was evacuated for three days. So, you see, while our children were gambolling among the daisies, befriending wild hedgehogs, filling their rosy cheeks with organic vegetables and so on, their old London muckers were camping out in a community hall somewhere in Acton, waiting for the bomb detectors to allow them back into their homes. It is impossible to communicate how smug that made us feel. How smug it continues to make us feel. And I need to hold on to that.

Because here we are, now, in our West Country idyll. Or here am I, to be more precise. The children are at school, the husband's in Soho, working.

My friends and colleagues are all in London, chatting away. And here I am in my West Country idyll, lungs bursting with fresh air and good will - and nobody to share it with. Except you. Reality is beginning to bite.

It's mid-morning. I've done the school run. I've admired the view from the sitting-room window; I've taken a turn around the utility room, and felt the usual little surge of pride. I've even ventured into the garden, albeit briefly. (It was a bit cold. Plus there was a slug.) I've checked the answer machine for messages. None. And the e-mail. None. I've taken another turn round the utility room, which, after nearly twenty years of hanging clothes on the banisters, never fails to soothe. And I've looked at my watch. Many times.

But heck, it's awful quiet around here.

And it will be, I suppose, until around lunch time, when the builders come. One of whom, by the way, is truly exorbitantly good looking. They - the handsome one and another one - are building us a kitchen in what used to be the second sitting room, and I keep popping in there in case the handsome one needs biscuits. Which he might, one time. He's always saying no. Yesterday morning I was sitting at my desk pretending to write, ears on stalks, biscuits at the ready, but he must have tiptoed into work extra quietly. The bastard. I never heard him come in.

Anyway, the point is, just because the handsome builder - and the other one - are more or less my only contact with the adult world these days, it doesn't mean I have nothing better to talk about. I do. I certainly do. Slug repellant, for example. According to my handsome builder, this little corner of the West Country is a national slug hotspot, with approximately 300 slugs for every square metre of earth. I've told him I have grand plans to make our own garden a one hundred per cent slug-free zone; I hinted I might even get Mr Osman and his bombs down here, if that's what it needed. I don't think he knew what I was talking about.

The truth is we've plopped ourselves in this beautiful corner of the world for all the right reasons; clean air/great schools/green fields/utility rooms. But - handsome builders aside - we don't know a soul. Our only hope of contact with the local world is at the school gate - the very place, for lots of mean-spirited reasons, I have always taken great care to avoid.

But beggars can't be choosers, can they? And there's a limit to how many nights a person can spend watching DVDs of *The West Wing*. I'm assuming. So come three o'clock (which, incidentally, is exactly three hours and twenty-one minutes away) I'll be slapping on my Stepford Grimace and standing at that school gate just like the rest of them: Desperately Pretending to be nicer than I am. Desperately Seeking a Social Life.

And it's going to be fine. In fact it's going to be better than fine. It's going to be *thrilling*. It's a whole new adventure.

Next Friday night, for example, the husband and I are booking a babysitter. We're getting ourselves all togged up in black tie and ball dresses, and heading off to our son and daughter's annual Parents' School Dance. Imagine the fun. If you will.

And I'm seriously looking forward to it.

January 15th

The tickets cost £50 each, including dinner, and the party took place in a room that looked and smelled a bit like my old school houseroom: the same mismatched, pastel-coloured walls, scuffed around the edges, and a pervasive stench of stale air, instant coffee and saliva. Actually it was the old town hall. One of the mothers, kind and welcoming as ever, had made enormous efforts to squeeze us onto her table and so I sat, adding to the festive odour, I suspect, with my very own hint of mothballs. I was underdressed in a strange pink rayon skirt and shirt ensemble, which has languished at the back of numerous wardrobes and storage boxes since I got it nearly twelve years ago. I have often wondered what possessed me to buy it in the first place – or why I ever insisted on keeping it. At least now I know that I'll never wear it again.

Fin and I set off for the party full of hope and good will. Fin caught an early train down and we arrived in perfect time. There was no milling about before dinner, which was good, really, since we neither of us had anyone to mill with. We were led straight away to our designated table. And things went pretty much downhill from there.

On either side of me sat a couple of men whose faces began to merge as the evening wore on. Both had moved with their families down from London (Chiswick) within the last ten years.

One worked in the City. He spent the week in a small flat in Hammersmith, and the weekend at home, catching up on some 'much-needed kip', and – presumably – having his shirts laundered for him by his wife.

'We find it works very well,' he said to me. 'It suits us. The kids are settled. We love the school. We love the lifestyle … I can really get my head down during the week. Which is super. And of course Katie's got her hands full with the kids!'

He asked me what my husband did for a living.

He had sandy-coloured hair and sandy eyelashes, a heavy metallic watch with sandy hairs encroaching, and an unyielding, incurious, slightly pudgy face. As, I'm pretty sure, did the man on the other side. But memory can play funny tricks. It's been a couple of days since I wrenched myself from their company, and I must admit I'm having some difficulty now distinguishing between the two.

The other man (I think) did not spend all week in London. On the contrary, he came down from his City job on Thursday nights, and spent Fridays working from home.

'We find it works very well,' he said to me. 'It suits us. The kids are settled. We love the school. We love the lifestyle … I can really get my head down during the week. Which is super. And of course Sarah's got her hands full with the kids!'

He asked me what my husband did for a living, and his goldfish eyes glazed over before I had time to reply.

I've never been very good at small talk. The truth is by the middle of the main course I had pretty much given up trying. One or other of the Sandy Men, in flirtatious mode, uttered a sentence which ended with the words 'ladies and all things technical!' and that was when I officially retired. The supreme pointlessness of our attempting to communicate any further became altogether overwhelming. My cheeks had lapsed into paralysis. My tongue had turned to lead. My heart was filled with resentment and boredom and I was thoroughly depressed. I had almost forgotten – if I'd ever even been aware – that men so unreconstructed actually existed. So I sat back and let them burble across me until coffee was served. They talked about Mercedes cars – their own and other people's – for the rest of the night.

At some point I looked across the table at Finley. He was faring better than I was, which wasn't really saying much. Some jolly old bird, squeezed into a strapless ball dress she should have chucked out back in 1983, was leaning across the table towards him, pressing her disco-dusted boobs together while he held out a light for her cigarette. She was having the time of her life, poor girl, oblivious to the scatter-gun approach of Fin's delightfulness, and glowing beneath his fantastic care. As he held out the flame she rested one of her hands on his arm. Her nails were freshly painted for the ball, I noted: dark plum, just like Uma Thurman's in *Pulp Fiction*, all those years ago. I caught F's eye. Noticed, beneath all the layers of delightfulness, an inescapable gleam of desperation there. It cheered me up enormously.

We danced after that, Fin and I. To a deafeningly loud and intermittently off-key rendition of FYC's 'She Drives Me Crazy'. And – it was kind of lovely. London seemed a long, long way away.

January 18th

The carpet layer is here. He shouldn't be, of course, because we still have a lot of building work to do; but he said he needed to shift the carpets quickly (storage space problems, apparently) which meant we either had to fit them this week or not fit them at all, and since his quote came in at £2,000 under everyone else's 'this week' seemed like the way to go. No doubt we shall come to regret it.

He's an obvious crook, by the way. Or he looks like one. Darrell suggested him. Darrell specifically advised me not to be put off by his appearance, but it's hard not to be. He has shifty eyes, one of which doesn't open properly, numerous studs and hoops in both ears, and a large, shaved head with a small swastika tattooed on top. Not that I care, so long as we get the carpets in, but his villainous appearance clearly troubles him. Every time he hears my feet in the hall he comes rushing out from whichever room he's measuring, and delivers another homily on integrity/importance of: especially in carpet layers. I nod like a puppy, of course. Nobody mentions the swastika.

In any case he's brought four teenage boys with him today, all of them a little damaged, by the look of things. Between them they have now removed all but one door in the house. There's a teenager calling himself Stewart, who doesn't seem to go in for eye contact, nor for the spoken word. But he obviously gets a hell of a lot of text messages, because for the last hour or so, while I've been working, he's been standing outside the hole where my office door used to be, deleting them one by one. And each time he deletes, it goes '*tring*', like he's waving a magic wand.

Which is of course reassuring, because at least it's proof that someone, somewhere, at some point, has been communicating with him. And not just once, but thousands and thousands and thousands of times. It means that maybe someone out there actually likes him. Or he's a drug dealer, of course. In any case he has a relationship with the world, and that has to be something to celebrate. Maybe he's not quite so damaged as he appears.

January 19th

Hatty called – for the first time in ages. I was giving the children a bath and I didn't get to the telephone on time. She left a message, sounding high as a kite, and not saying anything of any consequence really, except that her and Damian's five-minute film *Goodbye Jesus*, which has already won three minor awards at little film festivals around Europe …

Has just been nominated for an Oscar.

January 20th

Darrell stayed late this afternoon – late enough for me to offer him beer instead of the usual tea and biscuits. *Fantastic*, as Fin would say, while texting his location manager in Bucharest.

So I offered Darrell some beer, and he said yes! *Fantastic*. I think he fancies me. Maybe. A bit. Not nearly as much as I fancy him, obviously. But a little bit. Perhaps. Or he might do. I don't know.

Anyway it was just him and me, that's the thing. His partner (Ralph, I think??? He's OK but he has a nobbly head, like a bad potato; also, I suspect, beneath the friendliness, a simmering rage against toffs: both of which traits, for obvious reasons, I find a little off-putting.) His partner 'Ralph' had already left. Ditto the carpet layers. Ditto Mark the painter. Ripley and Dora were in the playroom entertaining themselves – and Fin is away. (Actually he's with his location manager in Bucharest, so no need for texting tonight. No need for worry either. Not on this occasion. She's young, but she's no beauty. Also, unusually stupid. I took the children to visit one of Fin's film sets a couple of years ago and we were introduced. 'H-E-L-L-O, M-U-M-M-Y!' she said to me, V-E-R-Y S-L-O-W-L-Y. And that was it. Amazing.)

Where was I? Darrell and me. Darrell *et moi* ... We talked about our travels in Florida. Darrell went to Orlando the year before last, but didn't manage to make it to Miami. He said he thought Orlando was mind-boggling. I said I thought so too, though truth be told I'm not convinced I've ever been there. I went to Jacksonville once, I think. In any case it didn't matter at all ... Florida has a lovely climate and a hell of a lot of alligators. We agreed on that. What else did we talk about?

I don't know. The kitchen, obviously. But I didn't want to focus on that. It would have put too much of an emphasis on – lots of things I didn't particularly want to emphasise at that particular moment. Anyway, I drank slightly more than half a bottle of wine in the time it took him to finish his two cans of lager – which, I think, is a slight improvement on the last time. I certainly wasn't reeling by the time he left, but I had taken up smoking again. Darrell smokes roll-ups. He offered to roll one for me. I know perfectly well how to roll my own, of course, but I decided not to mention it. I let him do the rolling and then I said *oooh*, because they did come out very neat. Oh dear. Oh dear.

Oh dear oh dear oh dear.

I can't help it. He's got such a fucking sexy laugh.

January 21st

Going to Clare Gower's coffee morning this morning.

Oddly enough I've never been to a 'coffee morning' before. Well, it's not that odd. Up until now I've made a fairly conscientious effort to avoid them. I have a nasty feeling this one may be quite a formal affair. Otherwise why would I have been invited to it almost a fortnight in advance?

She had to postpone the last one because she was having the outside of the house repainted, and she thought scaffolding might somehow 'confuse matters'. Not certain which matters, and I didn't like to ask. In any case the scaffolders have apparently packed up now, and taken with them all danger of confusion. The house is nicely repainted, Clare says, and the coffee morning is Back On. I have high hopes for it. Clare says she's expecting about ten guests – all women, of course. There must be one among them who might possibly be a friend?

I'm going upstairs now to put on some mascara in her honour.

COUNTRY MOLE

Sunday Times

———◆·◆———

There haven't been many times in my life when things have seemed so wretched that I really, truly wanted to press my own ejector seat and power into eternal space. But since leaving London for the West Country and a new existence of Healthy Family Fun, I find my fingers more often groping for the button.

Forget the pain of childbirth; the long, drawn-out death of a loved one; forget being eaten alive by piranha fish, or having a nail slowly hammered into the back of your neck. Hell is a coffee morning with the unemployed lady-mothers of idyllic rural Britain. Hell is knowing you stick out like a sore thumb and that you'll be stuck there, sticking out, for an hour minimum, smiling until your face cracks, before you can politely slip away again. Time hasn't passed so painfully since my last triple physics class, back in 1985. What a culture shock.

Nevertheless, I definitely tried to fit in. Said *mmmm* about the organic carrot and ginger nibbles, which were truly delicious; hooted with naughty laughter at the wicked 'willy' jokes, which were abysmal; managed (most impressively of all) to bite my tongue when they talked about their husbands' domestic predilections as if they were not only interesting but paramount, and left - a little early, admittedly, but full of gratitude and enthusiasm.

They saw through me. Maybe they could sense I didn't truly believe. At the school gate I bumped into the Hostess Lady-Mum, Queen Bee Lady-Mum, whose very delicious nibbles I'd *mmm'd* over so wholeheartedly, and I think she pretended not to see me. I sort of hopped this way and that, grinning, trying to catch her eye. She turned away. Somehow or other, I must have blown it.

In any case I shan't dwell on it. I mustn't obsess. They obviously all hate me, but I have to move on. It was a bad morning. A failed experiment. Suffice to say, the quest for a decent social life continues in earnest and I have decided once and for all that the ladies' coffee mornings are not, and never were, a realistic recruiting ground. Unless of course they happen to invite me again.

In the meantime I think I'd do better looking closer to home. At the builder, for example. Actually we have two builders, a painter, a landscape gardener and five carpet layers on the property as I write. I'm talking, of course, about the good looking one, the tea and biscuit-refusing installer of our new and exorbitantly tasteful, pale green kitchen, who sings Fred Astaire songs while he works, and who is, by the way, among the most handsome men I have ever met.

While the husband was hard at work in Bucharest

yesterday, the builder told me, in his lovely West Country burr, that he used to play a lot of tennis.

Well, blow my cotton socks off, and so did I!

In fact there's a run-down, faintly depressing old tennis club in the local town and I go there once a week in search of a match. So far I've not had any joy. It appears that everybody in the club already has 'their tennis organised'.

So it's with a mixture of desperation, loneliness and, obviously, lust that I've been trying to summon the nerve to ask him for a match. Trouble is – what if he thinks I'm propositioning him? Or – Christ, what if I *am* propositioning him? *Crickety-crackety*, what if he thinks I'm propositioning him and *he says Yes*?

OK. Obviously, that was silly. Over-excited and very, very silly. He's much too young for me. Apart from which, of course, we moved down here to be *more* of a family, not less: to pursue a life of good, clean, decent, honourable, innocent, monogamous fun. And that's what we're doing, dammit. For example, we went out in the woods yesterday, the children and I, and we built our very own bows and arrows. Out of natural sticks. God, it was fun! Or it would have been, except it was raining and the children wanted to watch telly and I was terrified about the slugs, and the arrows didn't really work and –

Anyway the main point is, I'm married.

February 1st

Well, here's a peculiar fact. Clare Gower, maker of immaculate ginger nibbles and agonisingly feeble willy jokes, has decided to overlook my spoddish performance at her coffee morning the other day. I was convinced she hated me, but it turns out she doesn't hate me at all. In fact she seems quite keen to become my friend.

Not because she likes me. She couldn't. We have nothing in common, beyond the whole life-cycle thing. I catch her looking at me sometimes with an expression of dull, vaguely pitying confusion. Nevertheless, in spite of that, in spite of my obviously being a misfit, something about me has obviously tickled her fancy. Or possibly she feels sorry for me. In any case she has invited Fin and me to a drinks party in three weeks' time *and* to a dinner party – not this Saturday, not the Saturday after that, nor the one after that, nor the one after that, nor, in fact, the one after that. But the next one. Though I know that under normal circumstances Clare and I would never dream of being friends, I am, of course, extremely happy and grateful for this new development.

Clare's pretty in an Alpen-eating, *Daily Mail*-reading kind of way: quite slim but not very, carefully dressed, with shoes and bags and nails and highlights and happy thoughts all nicely co-ordinated. She is always made up. Always tidy. Always smiling. And judging by her house (endlessly refurbished, late Georgian, with tennis court and swimming pool outside) she's pretty damn rich, too. Or her husband is. But above all, and in spite of her enthusiasm for swapping beauty secrets and a vaguely contemptible obsession with home décor, Clare is (and this is what I need to focus on) an incredibly *nice* woman; infinitely nicer, kinder, gentler, more patient and more generous-spirited than I will ever be.

Is she happy? That's the mystery. She's always perky – but it's hardly the same thing. She also doesn't have any frown marks. But that, she confided to a group of us the other day, is partly due to Botox and partly because for the past ten years she has slept every night in a special, tight-fitting rubber hat which stops her face from sagging. Also, she claims to sleep in a pair of lotion-infused fitted plastic gloves, which keep her hands looking young.

In any case she looks a lot younger than I do. And she's a very nice woman, and very kind, and anyway I reckon she's a better bet than Rachel White – who, incidentally, has finally managed to forgive Fin and me for that last-minute cancellation and has agreed to come to us for dinner. It's due to take place in about three weeks' time and I've warned her and her husband they'll be coming on their own, due to the fact that we don't know anyone else round here to invite them with. I suppose I could invite Clare (and husband), but I've seen the way Rachel looks at her, and I don't think they like each other very much.

February 5th

Hatty just called. She's told Damian to pack his bags. Turns out he's been having it off with his lead actress ever since they finished shooting back in November. The success of *Goodbye Jesus* has given Damian, for the first time in his wretched, bone-idle life, a certain amount of attention and success. And this is how he responds to it. *Quelle surprise*. What a wanker.

Hatty's wretched, needless to say. And very angry. All this time she's been paying for Damian and the director – so she thought – to fly around the world, promoting themselves at different film festivals. Little did she realise (until the director called her up to complain about it yesterday morning) that Damian's actually been leaving him at home in his Muswell Hill bedsit, and taking Tallullah Suckette – whatever the silly tart calls herself – instead.

Hatty and the children are coming down to Paradise for a couple of days to regroup. They should be arriving some time tomorrow.

Awful to say so – and I realise the circumstances aren't exactly ideal – but I'm really looking forward to it. Not to Hatty being miserable, obviously. But to the company.

Better get off to Waitrose then.

Busy, busy.

February 9th

I finally summoned the courage to ask Darrell if he fancied playing a game of tennis. I waited until Potato Head was out of the room and then I just spurted it out. It sounded very unnatural. Darrell turned round – he had his back to me, *hammering away* – and his expression wasn't unfriendly exactly, but he was obviously quite surprised. I gave a chirpy laugh, and I could feel myself blushing, and my head wobbling slightly, while I waited for him to respond. Which he didn't immediately. He put the hammer down and stretched across to turn off the radio and we looked at each other, me blushing, with the head wobbling this way and that.

'I'm quite good,' I said, to break the silence. Which I am. I mean *I am*. But he doesn't know that. Anyway, for the first time since I ever laid eyes on him I found myself slightly not fancying him, because after I said that his incredibly handsome face creased into an incredibly complacent smile. He laughed. He said, 'What do you want me to do? Play on one leg, shall I?'

I said he could play any way he wanted, if he believed it might help him – which I thought was quite quick. And he threw back his head and laughed so loud I spotted the new breakfast bar shaking. Which doesn't, I realise more clearly now, bode fantastically well for his handiwork. But it's not the point.

The kitchen's coming along fine, I'm sure. It looks lovely. It does, actually. It looks amazing. Like something out of *Interiors* magazine.

And we've made a date to play tennis this Friday afternoon. Fin's due home from London on the 8 o'clock train, which means – he's coming back at that time. Obviously.

And that's lovely, as it so happens. I've missed him a lot this week. The Commuter Widows at school endlessly assure me that, like them, I will get used to these long absences. And I suppose I will, when I turn into a nibble-baking, wrinkle-hat-wearing bloody Stepford robot like the rest of them.

Actually that's not quite what I meant.

What I meant was, for the moment I find I'm getting less accustomed to his absences every week rather than more, and – much as I despise myself for sliding into any kind of wifely cliché – increasingly resentful of his freedom to come and go as he pleases.

In any case, Darrell says that, regardless of how much work he has, he makes a rule of stopping at 3 o'clock on Fridays. Which is news to me. Not that I care. Far from it. I'm in no rush for him to finish his work here. At all. In fact, I worry he's getting through it all a bit too quickly. So I'm going to arrange for the children to have tea with their school friends on Friday, and Darrell and I are going to shimmy down to that tennis club together.

I think it's about time I bought some new sportswear.

… And perhaps a short spell on a sunbed, if can find one somewhere …

Hatty cancelled in the end. She texted me just after I'd hauled the final shopping bag up the hill from Waitrose. She said at the last minute she had to go to Frankfurt. Some crisis at work, apparently. I hope she's all right. Her mobile's been switched off and I haven't managed to speak to her since.

February 10th

God, this house is cold. Why's it always so cold? Every room in this bloody house seems to have a howling gale blasting through it. I've got three jerseys on and a sodding *vest* and I still can't get warm …

Anyway. Column day today. Only my third instalment and already beginning to get nervous about it. Nobody's mentioned the coffee morning article. I don't think the ladies really read newspapers around here. Or not the big ones. But what if they did? Would Clare Gower be able to recognise herself? Would she? Christ, I hope not. A couple of times, at the school gate, when I've been talking to her and the others, I get a flash of something I've written – or, worse, of something I'm going to write – and I feel sick. Sick with my own duplicity and viciousness. How can I do it? How can I be so mean? But then the next minute, there I am, in front of the computer, and the adrenalin's going – I find my imagination going into overdrive and I can't resist.

So – what am I going to write about this week? That won't make me feel sick with self-loathing the moment after I've filed it?

COUNTRY MOLE

Sunday Times

⇒•⇐

Our eldest child, Dora, who's eight, has been cam-
paigning for a life surrounded by green fields since
long before there was any serious suggestion we might
move out of London. In Shepherds Bush, where her bedroom overlooked three vast, grey, BBC satellite dishes and a multi-storey car park, she used to sit on
her bed and draw pictures of houses in green fields
with eight-year-old girls living inside them.

Today, in our new house, she has fields directly
behind the house. So that's good. The lady wanted
fields. We got them for her. That's how modern families work. Except yesterday, when I suggested she
might actually go and play in them, Dora replied: 'It
turns out fields are a bit boring.' And it's not that
I want to kill her or anything, because I don't.
Obviously. But there was another house, which didn't
have fields. And we chose this one instead. It's the
last time I ever give her what she wants. Ever. She's
getting a tin of slug repellant for her birthday,
whether she likes it or not. It turns out no girl can
ever have too much of that.

The other house, without the fields, was £50,000

cheaper, I'm remembering now. It had a nice flat garden and a kitchen already built. And it wasn't 'uniquely positioned' either, as our imaginative estate agent chose to put it. The house we live in now is so uniquely positioned I doubt we'll ever be able to sell it again. It perches on a slope so sheer that we can't get the car to the front door. To reach the house, we have to park about 70 foot below, clamber up 33 steps (each one counted, often) and over a slippery, winding, unlit garden path, where there may be giant slugs and murderers lurking. All of which seemed droll and refreshingly rustic when we first spotted the place that distant, sun-dappled day back in May.

At some point, to be fair, I did ask the previous owners if the lack of any sensible access had proved much of an inconvenience. They looked at me as if I was mad. They were quite horrible people, as a matter of fact. A tight little family of cold fish, strangely snooty and addicted to all things taupe. In any case they were adamant, in their snooty way, that the heart-palpitating scramble required to reach their own front door had barely registered on their consciousness, and they told me so with such disdain - all three of them: mummy, daddy and the spooky eighteen-year-old - that I felt quite silly having brought up the subject at all.

I've since learned (from a friend of their former neighbour) that the problem used to keep them awake at nights. They had submitted plans, all refused by the council, to build underground garages into the face of the hill, with a linking subterranean tunnel to the front door. Or something along those lines. So they were being a little economical with the *actualité*, on top of all their other crimes – their appalling addiction to beige, their lack of books or senses of humour …

But so it goes. All's fair in love and real estate. The kitchen ceiling's on the point of collapse. Ditto what's left of the guttering. Ditto the vaulted cellar room, built into the hill of the back garden. There is no water in the children's bathroom; the central heating doesn't work properly; the supporting beams in the roof are riven with woodworm; and it turns out the entire county is infested with giant slugs. But none of it matters. Or mattered then. We loved the house from the first viewing. Its snooty owners might have thrown themselves to the ground and sobbed for hatred of their impregnable hill and the fact that their entire, uniquely positioned house was almost certainly in the process of sliding down it. The truth is we wouldn't have listened.

February 14th

Hatty's being a bit odd. I think she may have a lover already, or maybe she's had one all along and she's not telling me about it. Which is a bit mean. She seems weirdly unphased by the end of her marriage. Also a bit shifty. Finally talked to her this morning – the first time since she told me it was all over between Damian and her – and she sounded almost pissed off when she discovered it was me calling. She couldn't wait to get me off the line. Also – incapable of talking about anything except the bloody Oscars. She and the director are going out to LA together, she says. They're staying in the Chateau Marmont, and, tee hee hee, they're leaving Damian behind.

Just noticed it's Valentine's Day.

February 21st

Darrell reckons he and the Potato Man will be more or less finished here by this time next week. He says they have to be finished anyway, because they have a big job starting immediately afterwards, and then another job lined up straight after that. I think we were very lucky to get him – them – when we did. Sod's law, though, isn't it? He's the first builder in the history of builders to finish a job when he says he will, and I don't even want him to. The kitchen looks amazing; stunning – but … But. But. I've lost all interest in amazing-looking kitchens suddenly. In fact I'm not sure if I ever really had any.

We played the tennis. I don't suppose we'll play again. I mean I want to, obviously, but the truth is, if he hadn't been so lovely about it the whole thing might have been a bit embarrassing. Because he wasn't just good – and 6 foot 3 – he was brilliant. Turns out he used to play for the county, which I rather wish he'd mentioned earlier, and in two humiliating sets I won exactly four points off him, three of which I'm almost certain were sympathy points. The match was finished within twenty minutes of getting on court. I was pouring with sweat. All I really wanted was to stagger into the nearest dung heap and sob, really. Nevertheless, courageously, I insisted on pretending to be up for a third set.

Luckily he didn't. In fact he laughed when I suggested it. He said he'd much prefer to buy me a drink in the pub opposite instead.

We spent nearly three hours in there. The children were both staying over with friends, and Fin wasn't due in at the train station until evening, and the pub was pretty dark and pretty quiet, and we had a corner table by the fire – and I smoked his roll-ups and we both got pretty pissed on cider. And he was lovely. He asked me questions as if he was genuinely interested in the answers, in a way that allowed me to answer them straight – without feeling the need to be clever, for once. He talked about his work and about singing, because he has a beautiful voice, and about poetry, briefly, because it turns out, oddly, that he reads a lot of it. (I don't, of course, but because of being a writer and so on I felt under some pressure to bluff. So I dredged through memories of my English A-level revision notes and announced that I particularly admired John Donne. Darrell didn't. I couldn't remember a single thing Donne had ever written, so the conversation didn't last long.) We also talked about tennis – he told me about the day he was picked out by a talent scout who came to his primary school. He told me about his sister, who has two children and no husband and who is training to be a nurse, and about his mother, who ran off to Spain when he was seven, and who he's only seen a couple of times since. He told me about his dad dying, and about his four-year-old son, conceived during a whirlwind two-month romance with a girl called Denise.

He told me he was divorced.

And that was when – For God's sake. Nothing happened. Nothing bloody well happened. And it never would have done. But I suppose – I don't know – there was just a moment, maybe, when the clamour dimmed, briefly, and we liked each other. We really *liked* each other, and we were just two people, without all the baggage. And after he told me he was divorced there was a fairly obvious pause, quite a long fairly obvious pause, and I, for one, started imagining the two of us in bed.

He said, quite quietly, with that incredibly low, soft voice of his, 'What time's the old man getting in?' And it snapped me right back into the present. Finley's train was due in any minute. I'd been meaning to go back to the house and pick up the car, but a) it was too late now, and b) I was too drunk to drive. So Darrell gave me a lift to the station in his van. We didn't really speak on the journey. The spell was broken. The clamour was back. At the station I leapt out of the van as if the seat had been burning my bottom. I made some stupid, chirpy, facetious comment about our next tennis match, and he laughed his lovely baritone laugh, and he drove away.

And there was Fin. Looking good, actually. I forget how good looking he is sometimes. And he was laughing and smiling and pleased to be back, and I was so happy to see him I almost – bloody nearly – cried. And I never cry. How pathetic is that? In any case we had a lovely long, cold walk back to the house, a lovely, warm evening together without the children. And then, when the children got home on Saturday morning, a really happy weekend. We took them to look for frog-spawn down by the stream, but I think it may be the wrong time of year for it, because we didn't find any. The four of us hardly argued at all.

And now Fin's gone back to London, the children are at school, Potato Head has gone on to another job, and Darrell's in the kitchen, *hammering away*. He's singing along to an Elvis Presley song on the radio, but not as joyfully as usual, I think. I made him a cup of tea this morning and I've been avoiding him ever since. We haven't quite looked each other in the eye all day.

What a mess. What a shame. What a nuisance life is.

I have nothing to do now but school runs and writing, until Friday evening, when Fin returns from his week away, and we are expected for drinkipoos with Clare Gower. What fun.

But perhaps if I hang around at the school gate for long enough tomorrow morning, someone might invite me over for a cup of coffee.

February 22nd

Bingo! Rachel White spotted me lingering hopefully, pretending to look for my car keys just outside Ripley's classroom, and she asked me if I had timeforacoffee.

I could have hugged her. *Timeforacoffee?*

Time for a *thousand* cups of coffee, Rachel! What shall we talk about?

Let's talk about *sex*, baby.

Let's talk about you and me.

And *eugenics*. And *Trident*. And *habeas corpus* …

We went to the Coffee Bean – a nice coffee shop, which is attached to the main gift shop on the high street, where the parking is quite convenient, and it was great. *Fantastic,* as Fin would say. We just nattered away as if we'd known each other all our lives. Simple as that. I apologised a couple more times about the dinner cancellation – which apologies she graciously accepted – and I reiterated how much we were both looking forward to the rescheduled dinner back at ours, next week.

Then we talked about how Rachel sometimes persuades, sometimes cajoles and sometimes, when she's desperate, even hoodwinks Martin (6 yrs) and Jenny (10 yrs) into eating an assortment of appetising vegetables each mealtime. We also talked about which vegetables Jenny preferred and which ones Martin preferred and whether girls naturally preferred more vegetables than boys or whether that was only particular to Martin (6) and Jenny (10), since Jenny (10) tended to be more partial to more vegetables, e.g. broccoli and Brussels sprouts, which she calls 'baby cabbages', than her brother (6), who doesn't seem to like any vegetables at all, except raw carrots, which he will usually be willing to eat, but only if Mummy ($39^1/_2$) cuts them into animal shapes, and he's allowed to dip them into organic tomato ketchup.

Two more days until Fin comes home. The boiler's broken in his office so he's abandoned the new sofabed for a bed somewhere a little more comfortable. He's staying at Hatty's.

Which is fine.

Clare Gower just called to postpone the drinks. She says she's having the front of the house reterraced. It was meant to have been finished by Friday but it's not going to be now, and the whole place, she says, is so muddy, it looks 'like a very muddy war zone'. Shame. I was looking forward to it, actually. Anyway, the poor girl sounded distraught, almost in tears, so I've invited her to come and have lunch with me next week. I think, to be honest, it cheered us both up a little bit. She's always so friendly, always laughing and chatting away at the school gate, but there's something about her – beneath all the tinted moisturizer and so on – which seems kind of lost, and a little lonely. Or perhaps I just have loneliness on the mind.

In any case, we're having lunch together next week, and though the drinks party is now postponed the dinner party still stands, and is due to take place in late March. The 24th, I think. Things are definitely hotting up.

February 24th

Friday. I'm on the train, on a day trip to London, and I've left Fin in Paradise on his own – for the first time. I feel light-headed with the freedom: I have a work lunch first (justification for the trip), then I'm going shopping. And then it's drinks at E&O with two of my best friends. (Not Hatty. Who didn't bother to ring back when I called up to suggest it.) And then it's back to Paradise on the last train.

Fin and I have Rachel Healthy-Snax White and her husband coming to dinner on Saturday night. Fin says he'll go to Waitrose this afternoon. Plus he came home with flowers last night. He does do that sometimes, because (when he's around) he's lovely. He is … fantastic. Sometimes even better than that. Nevertheless. I think he must be feeling a bit guilty because he also bought me a beautiful bracelet from – Ooh. Text message from Darrell! Do I want to play tennis with him next week?

Do I?

COUNTRY MOLE

Sunday Times

———◆◆———

Clearly I'm not the only one who is desperate for a social life around here. I escaped to London one day last week, was browsing blissfully through the racks at TK Max in Hammersmith when my mobile rang and a husky, feminine voice, faintly familiar, demanded without the slightest preamble whether a woman's name, quite well known, happened to 'mean anything' to me.

I thought it was some old journalist friend, being slightly affected and pretending to be on such a pressing deadline that she didn't have time for pleasantries. So I played along, always delighted to have my expertise referred to:

'She's an actress,' I said briskly. 'Or she was. Very beautiful and glamorous and all that, but she got a bit Green after she married. Gave a lot of interviews about not flushing the lavatory. Why? Who is this anyway?'

'Well, yes.' The sexy voice faltered slightly. 'That's … It's me. I mean … I meant. I was talking about me.'

'It's you?' *Very odd*, I thought. *Also quite*

embarrassing. 'Hello. What a nice surprise.'

'I think we met ... a long time ago. But perhaps we didn't. Actually I don't think we did.'

'Oh, gosh, no, yes I'm sure we did,' I said, very quickly. 'Hello! How lovely! Gosh, how are you? It's been ... I mean seriously it's been ages.'

'Well maybe we met,' she said impatiently. 'Maybe we did, maybe we didn't. In any case ...'

She'd been given my number by a mutual friend, who moved to live in the country several years ago and who has recently bought herself a couple of Hereford cows for company. Which isn't a great sign, now I come to think of it. In any case the sexy, glamorous non-lavatory-flushing actress lived about an hour away from our own West Country idyll. And she wanted to know if my husband and I would be free to come to dinner the following Saturday.

Is this normal, outside London? Is it? To cold-call people while they're shopping in TK Max and ask them out to dinner? I was delighted, of course.

Would have accepted at the drop of a hat. Would have made sure I went to the lavatory before I left, to avoid any chance of an ugly scene. But, hell, I'm going to jump at any opportunity to alleviate a fellow exile's sense of isolation. Obviously.

It made me wonder, though whether there aren't quite a few of us stranded out here: dyed-in-the-wool metropolitans, feeling lonely and lost in our relentlessly green and pleasant landscapes. Perhaps there are. Maybe I should set up some kind of a website.

In any case, tragically (not to say freakishly) my husband and I already have a social arrangement for that night. And not one shipped in from London, either. In fact we have a couple of *bona fide* locals coming to call! Which, clearly, is something to celebrate.

Ages ago one of the Mothers at school very kindly asked the husband and I to a dinner party, and – needless to say – I accepted the invitation with all the gratitude and enthusiasm it deserved. For several weeks before the big event, as we waited for our children at the gate, she and I would talk about it. She said she intended to invite several neighbours, whom she believed the husband and I would get along with. She also asked, at least twice, whether either of us was vegetarian.

But the dinner never happened, for reasons too complicated to explain. Suffice to say our metropolitan approach to last-minute cancellations (husband's fault, not mine) caused untold offence and it took quite a lot of quite hefty spadework on my part to make amends – the consequence of which spadework is that on the night in question she and her husband have finally agreed to come to dinner at ours.

All well and good. Peace reigns in Paradise once again.

But it means there will be no merry cavorting with the glamorous and lonely for us. Not on that occasion. We shall be entertaining Mrs Healthy-Snax, who only likes to talk about getting her children to eat vegetables, and Mr Healthy-Snax, of course, whose real name I once knew but which I have now sadly forgotten.

The last time I saw him was on a freezing, miserable afternoon just before Christmas. I was feeling particularly depressed at the time – so depressed, I could barely muster eye contact with my steering wheel, let alone with the human race. But there he was, *ragging around* on the school playing field, dressed in rugby shirt and Santa hat, and treating the Reception class to an impromptu lesson in ball control. Or something. It took all my self-control not to run him over.

But anyway that was then.

I'm sure it's all going to be great fun.

Monday February 27th

Which is worse? Talking to Rachel Healthy-Snax White about kidz'n'vegetables for an entire Saturday evening, or running out of beauty secrets to share with Clare Gower at the school gate, or discovering that Johnny Depp, not spotted in Waitrose for several weeks now, has in fact just bought an island off Hawaii? Which is worse – all that, or to be screaming at the dog for shitting in the playroom again, and simultaneously to be receiving a text from Fin telling me that Hatty, my best friend, currently in Los Angeles, just rung him (currently in Barcelona) to tell him that *Goodbye Jesus* won the Oscar for Best Short Film last night.

Which is worse?

And I still haven't decided what to reply to Darrell.

Clare's coming to lunch on Friday, so I've bought a copy of *In Style* magazine to prepare. Dora and I have been swatting over it all weekend. Extremely enjoyable it was too. Turns out I've been Stuck in a Style Rut for ages now, and so has Dora. I have promised to take Dora on a day trip to the Primark in Hammersmith one day very soon, because I feel her Style Rut might be more easily and cheaply remedied than my own. Everything she wears looks beautiful on her, even when it costs £2 from Primark. It would be impossible to say which of us is looking forward to the trip more. I'm almost tempted to pull her out of school for it.

Rachel Healthy-Snax and her husband Jeremy Healthy-Snax came to supper on Saturday night. As expected, they were not very interesting.

I had tried to forewarn Finley, who's done almost no socialising in Paradise yet, that he needed to be on his mettle, that the evening was not going to be a breeze, and that he was likely to encounter difficulties maintaining concentration as the night wore on. But he didn't listen. Actually he snarled at me. He said *I* was the boring one, for always being so negative about new people. Then he said, as the doorbell was ringing (promptly, at 8.01 on the button): 'It is possible, you know, *not* to live in Notting Hill Gate and *not* to write novels or work in the media, and still to be an extremely interesting person. I'll bet Rachel and Jeremy are fascinating. In their own way. The problem isn't them, it's *you*, because you are such an *intolerant, narrow-minded, bitchy, metropolitan snob ...*'

Wanker. What the hell's Notting Hill got to do with it anyway? Only bankers live in Notting Hill these days. As he knows perfectly well.

So the evening got off to a good start, with both of us spitting at each other as we tripped off to open the front door.

And then Fin, who's been working very hard recently, fell fast asleep in the middle of pudding.

He might almost have got away with it too, funnily enough. I'm not sure our guests would have noticed, they were so busy chatting away. Except he suddenly let rip with a table-shaking, deep-throated, nasal-passage-grouting snore. *Disgusting.* And it was just as our guest, Jeremy Healthy-Snax, was reaching the climax of his story about a chap at Paradise train station who had the same briefcase as his, even though he – Jeremy – had bought his at Geneva airport. So. The timing was unfortunate. Jeremy had been expecting laughter, maybe a murmur of surprise, perhaps even a follow-on question:

What took you to Geneva, Jeremy? Business or ski-ing?

Instead he got Finley. Being rude and disgusting at the same time. Rachel and Jeremy were both pretty shocked. They pretended to laugh, but I could see that their feelings and their sense of decorum were both quite seriously offended. They left soon afterwards, pretty much immediately after coffee.

So that's them. I dunno. I'm annoyed, really, and embarrassed – because maybe they're never going to be our friends. They're obviously never going to be our friends, but they're OK. *In their own way*. There was no need for Fin to offend them. Again. Especially after that conceited lecture about intolerance and Notting Hill Gate.

Fin and I had a humdinger of a row after they were gone.

Tuesday February 28th

Can't concentrate on anything this morning. I can't. I'm so behind with my work but I just can't concentrate. Why did Hatty call Fin about the stupid Oscar before she called me? Why? Why would she do that? What's going on between those two, and also, is it my imagination or are they being peculiarly unsubtle about it? Either they're both very stupid, which they aren't. Or they're trying to fool me with a double bluff. Or I'm going insane.

Which I'm not. I don't think.

Fin's called three times so far today but I haven't spoken to him yet. In fact I haven't spoken to him since he flew to Barcelona on Sunday night. And Hatty's left a message from Los Angeles. I'm usually so desperate for someone to talk to I call them both back straight away. But now all I can think about is him and Hatty, *Hatty and him* – and I'm in such a stew about it I don't quite trust myself to speak to either of them.

Also, bloody Mabel, not content with peeing on Ripley's bed while he was sleeping in it last night, this morning decided it would be fun to chew through my computer's power cable. I sincerely hope it gave her an electric shock, because the battery's now flat, and due to the computer's enormous age (four years) there is no replacement cable for sale anywhere within a 200-mile radius of Paradise. I'm having to get one sent from London. They say it's going to take at least a week.

Which means, unless I write longhand, as I am now – but it's not the same – any real progress on the novel, today exactly a fortnight overdue, is going to be pretty much out of the question. The next column isn't due in for nine days, thank God. And I suppose it's lucky I haven't got any other journalism on at the moment. Haven't had any for ages, now I come to think of it. In fact the calls from all my usual commissioning editors seem to have completely dried up. Why?

Sod it. I think I'll take Ripley and Dora to McDonalds for tea. I've been in such a foul mood since I fetched them from school earlier. Perhaps it'll cheer us all up.

Tuesday night

Children got quite annoyed with me this evening, even in spite of the McDonald's treat. Don't blame them, either. I wasn't listening to a word they were saying, poor things. I was responding to everything on 100 per cent automatic – and then Ripley was waving a free piece of plastic junk in front of my nose and shouting something at me, and at the same instant I had a picture of Hatty and Fin going at it hammer and tongs, and I snapped. Flicked the piece of plastic out of my face so it flew half way across the restaurant. 'For *God's sake, SIT DOWN*,' I yelled – but he was sitting. Perfectly. His face crumpled and Dora put her arm around him.

'He's only showing you something,' she said. 'What's so wrong with that? And all you're doing is just *existing* to be sorry for yourself.'

Funny, when the things you say get mixed around and thrown back at you. She certainly had a point. So I apologised. Went to retrieve the bloody plastic from under some obese young mother's foot, but it was already broken.

'Doesn't matter,' said Ripley, very bravely. 'I think it was already broken anyway.'

We ate mostly in silence for a while after that. I felt guilty. Made a few attempts to ignite a to-and-fro on matters traditionally suitable for children, as I always do when I realise I've been useless. I begin to patronise them.

Did Mrs Sprott, I asked Ripley, think the boys or the girls were better at keeping their tuck boxes tidy?

Ripley and Dora exchanged glances over their filthy hamburgers and started giggling. 'Mum, just because you pinged that toy,' Dora said, 'doesn't mean you have to be *boring*.'

Which took the pressure off. We cheered up quite a lot after that.

Text message.

It's Darrell ... At ten o'clock. Says he's just got back from work! Also that he's passing near by the house this Friday lunchtime with a couple of hours to spare and he's still hoping for 'that' game of tennis. Was there ever a 'that' game? I don't remember – after the humiliation of the last one I can't imagine daring to suggest ever playing him again. Or maybe I did. It doesn't matter, anyway. God, what a –

Oh dear. Sounds like Ripley's crying. And he's yelling at Mabel. Again. He's *got* to stop putting her in bed with him at night. Poor Ripley. Better go.

Wednesday

Just ordered some modern, exciting new kitchen chairs to match our modern, exciting, newly finished kitchen. Only seen a picture of them on the internet so far, and they're suspiciously cheap, but never mind. They're supposed to be delivered next week.

March 2nd

Hatty left a message on the mobile last night, sounding slightly offended, which I thought was a bit rich. She said she 'presumed' that I'd heard The News. Well of course

I've heard The News. She very thoughtfully rang my husband in Barcelona to tell him about it. Anyway, I've decided not to return the call until I'm feeling a bit calmer. Or until I know what the hell is going on. Or until I stop feeling like a mad, jealous bitch. Or something.

I've not talked to Fin all week – at least not properly. We made a couple of attempts at conversation on Wednesday, but he always sounded distracted, and then, both times, he cut me off mid amazingly interesting anecdote, because something more important came up. So. He's called back several times since then, but I'm not interested. I've been ignoring him. Trouble is I'm not sure he's noticed yet.

Also, annoyingly, I'm dying to talk to him about the neighbours' secret tree planting. I've only just noticed what's been going on.

In all the time we've been here there's been very little sign of life from the big house next door. It's not next door, actually, it's about 20 metres down the hill. Or 100 metres – I don't know. Close enough to be able to see if they've left a window open, but nowhere near close enough (disappointingly) to be able to hear what's being said inside. Our house is further up the hill than theirs, slightly smaller and a great deal scruffier; inferior, in fact, in every aspect but its proximity to the stars. It means, obviously, that we're fitter, due to the extended scramble required to reach our front door; also that from numerous rooms in our scruffy house we enjoy an interrupted view, not only of Paradise, but of their big, fat, perfect but not especially interesting back garden.

I have never seen anyone playing in it. In fact, apart from the time I spotted a young man in overalls, regrouting a wall, I have never seen anyone in it at all. Which is quite odd, because it's vast, and there's not a weed in it anywhere. So somebody has to be spending a hell of a lot of time out there looking after it. But when? For some reason they must only be willing to come out at night.

In any case, country neighbours are supposed to be friendly, aren't they? I thought they were supposed to welcome newcomers with baskets of vegetables and invitations to pop round for soup. Not these ones. I went over to introduce myself once, soon after it became obvious they were never going to do it themselves. The windows were open but they didn't answer the doorbell, and something about the place – it's immaculate lifelessness – gave me the jitters. I didn't hang around. Since then, one way or another, there has always been a vaguely mysterious, vaguely hostile cloud wafting silently between our two houses. I have sensed it. I have been sure of it. But until now I never had any proof.

Somehow – under cover of night perhaps – they have secretly planted a line of young trees along the wall between our two gardens. Not only that: the postman says they're a breed of tree which usually grows at least 10 foot every spring.

Friday 4th

Arrived back from the school run this morning to discover that the beautiful horsehair ceiling, with all its intricate, ancient, delicate, irreplaceable plaster moldings, has collapsed – directly onto our brand new, pale green kitchen.

And here I am, doing absolutely nothing about it. I'm lying on my bed, writing my diary.

When I came in just now and I first saw the absolute wreck which, however briefly, was possibly the smartest kitchen in the whole of the South West of England – and then I looked up and saw the socking great hole in what, for almost 200 years, was possibly the most elegant ceiling in Paradise – I laughed. I don't know why. I just laughed until there were tears pouring down my cheeks. Freaked me out a bit.

I suppose I was struck, suddenly, by the utter silliness of everything: the whole bloody Project: of Fin and me ever imagining we could create this perfect house, this perfect life. How greedy and naïve we have been. How arrogant and vain and altogether fatuous. It seemed funny. I think. For a moment. Because now the bathroom's collapsed onto the kitchen, the countryside's covered in slugs, the children think fields are boring, Daddy never bothers to come home any more and

Mummy's on the point of copping off with the builder …

No. She's not.

Either way, we're going to have to find a new builder from somewhere, I suppose, and not because of the *frisson*, either. I happen to know that Darrell's got too much work on as it is. There's not a chance he'd have time to do it. And, for the moment at least, I don't care. As far as this house is concerned, I've run out of puff. There's a sink in the laundry room, and a table in the playroom, and after I've picked up the children maybe we can go to Argos and buy a little microwave oven. I'm going to close the doors on kitchen and bathroom – or what's left of them both – and ignore that whole section of house until Fin gets back. He can deal with it. And in the meantime, with or without the bloody computer cable, I have got to get on with some work.

Unless Darrell drops by. Obviously. Which I suppose he might, it being Friday and all. Incidentally I've formed quite a good strategy re Darrell. One which puts me morally in the clear, which is important, but on the other hand doesn't rule anything out, which would be needlessly depressing, especially under the circumstances. I have decided not to reply to his texts – not to the two he's already sent, nor even if he texts me again … Which means I could hardly accuse myself of encouraging him. On the other hand if he does happen to turn up, with a racquet in his hand and so on, then … well … What will be, will be. Tennis it is. Or whatever. Tennis it isn't. What will be, will be.

March 7th

Fin caught the early train to London this morning, armed with a lot of telephone numbers for local builders. He said he would dedicate the entire journey to finding somebody to fix the kitchen ceiling. He said that, and neither of us could be bothered to point out what we both knew – that he could dedicate as much journey time as he liked: the mobile signal is so bad on that route it's virtually impossible to make a single call without getting cut off. I spent two hours once, trying to remind the painter not to let the dog out. By the time I reached Paddington I must have dialled him fifteen times without getting the message across. And Mabel, of course, was long gone. She didn't turn up again until the following morning. So. Anyway. In the meantime efforts – such as they are – to rebuild the new kitchen proceed at a dead snail's pace, i.e. not at all, and I don't mind in the least. It's a good excuse not to do any cooking.

No more texts from Darrell. Which is probably a very good thing. Actually the doorbell rang last Friday, when I was still lying there writing the diary, and I was a bit worried by my reaction to it. I sprang off the bloody bed as if I'd just been electrocuted. And the very first thought that crossed my mind, even before I landed, wasn't, for example:

'Perhaps that's the new computer cable come to save my bacon,' or: 'Perhaps that's the furniture shop, come to drop off my suspiciously cheap new chairs.' It was:

HE'S HERE! *What pants have I got on?*

In any case, he wasn't HERE at all. It was Clare Gower, arrived for lunch. But what with the kitchen ceiling falling in I had completely forgotten she was coming.

She couldn't have been more sympathetic, more tactful, more understanding or more forgiving. When she saw the state of the new kitchen she almost burst into tears. She said she couldn't even bear to look at it and we had to retreat to the sitting room for her to recover.

As soon as she'd done that, she put in a call to her own builders.

'They should jump at it,' she muttered, tappety-tapping onto the mobile with her lovely, tidy, shiny nails. 'The amount we spend with them, they should offer to do it for free! They're ever so nice, though. They always leave the place super-tidy afterwards. So don't worry.' She glanced at me. 'Soon as I've done this,' she said, 'I'm taking you out to lunch. No arguing. So off you pop upstairs and change.'

So – Well. I dunno. Didn't have anything else to do. And there wasn't any food in the house. Off I popped.

When I came downstairs, this time in a cleaner pair of jeans and wearing mascara, Clare looked me up and down and managed not to frown, just about. 'Much better!' she said unconvincingly. 'Right then! Off we go! And before you say anything, this one's on me. And I'm driving!'

It turned out her builders were booked up until well

beyond the next ice age. So that was that. We forgot the kitchen, as soon as she allowed us to, and headed out to lunch. She drove us to a pretty pub about twenty minutes away, which had a lot of Range Rovers parked outside, and a menu as good or better than most places in London and – honestly – it was a treat. Don't think I'd realised how gloomy I was feeling until Clare cheered me up again. We talked about beauty secrets, of course. I confided to her the truth of Dora's and my Style Rut, and she suggested I drop in at Chanel next time I was in London. She said her husband, Roger, bought her something from Chanel every Christmas and every birthday, and that it was definitely her favourite shop. She especially loved the packaging. We discussed the health and beauty benefits associated with drinking plenty of water, and I learned that fizzy water has been known to increase cellulite. We talked about Farrow and Ball paints now being available in Homebase. And we politely took it in turns to relate adorable anecdotes about our children.

We both grew steadily tipsier. I mentioned the neighbours and their evil wall of trees. She said she knew them vaguely; and though Clare doesn't say negative things about anyone I got the distinct impression she didn't like them. She certainly didn't want to talk about them anyway.

After the third glass of wine she asked me how I was settling in Paradise, and I confided in her that with Fin away and no friends around I was finding it 'difficult'. Wish I hadn't said it now. Too bad.

In any case, she leant forward and there was, I think,

between the carefully blackened eyelashes, a flicker of something less perky than usual: of fear, perhaps – or perhaps that was always there – perhaps of understanding. She said very quickly, very quietly … that after five years a commuter widow in Paradise there were still times when she *got a bit fed up*, too.

And that was it. Then she changed the conversation.

She knows a woman who comes to the house with her own St Tropez tanning machine, she says, and she's thinking of organising a ladies' St Tropez night at her house, for all the mums. I said I thought that it sounded like great fun.

COUNTRY MOLE

Sunday Times

It's possible that my eternally absent husband, who works in the film industry, has always led a fractionally more glamorous existence than I have. But since we moved to Paradise the difference between our two lifestyles has become embarrassing. Take today, for example. He is in Barcelona, or so he tells me, having lunch with Antonio Banderas. He's just texted me that the sun is shining and that 'Antonio' is being delightful. Which is good.

Down here in Paradise, meanwhile, I have taken the dog for a bracing walk and torn the pocket of my anorak, trying to squeeze through a barbed-wire fence. So. When the husband calls tonight, that'll be the hot news. The anorak. Followed seamlessly by whatever the hell I might have cooked the children for din-dins.

Actually if things don't liven up a bit I may have to duck the call altogether. I have some pride left, and there was a time when I definitely used to be interesting. So, yes, I'll screen the call. Keep him guessing what those children had for din-dins, dammit! And in the meantime I can only hope that

while I'm busying myself with bracing walks and broken anoraks, some delicious Barcelona starlet isn't
busying herself with – never mind.

Forget it.

I've been thinking a lot about trees lately, the
way we country folk do.

Now that spring is supposed to be coming I find
myself especially concerned with a row of young
saplings recently planted in my unknown neighbour's
immaculately tended garden. The trees are still
small. I'm fairly certain they weren't even planted
until after we bought the house. Or if they were, we
didn't notice them, and nor, by the way, did the
postman. We (the husband, the postman and I) were all
too bowled over by the spectacular view; which view,
and this is my point, those innocent-looking saplings
are soon going to completely obliterate.

And there in a nutshell is the trouble with rural
living. Yes, you can leave your flak jacket on its peg
in the hall, and no, there are no pools of drunken
vomit between your car and the front door. But which
inner-city dweller has ever had to lie awake at night
worrying about the growth rate of poplar saplings?
Because if those little poplars are left to flourish
unhindered they could knock tens of thousands off the
value of our property. They could send us spiralling
into negative equity, trapping us in this godforsaken
Paradise for ever …

I asked our very friendly postman for advice,
because he always pauses to admire the view/catch his

breath when he comes up here. He suggested putting an end to the trees by climbing the wall one night and hammering brass tacks into their roots. Simple enough. And very hard to detect, apparently. We'd almost certainly get away with it. Yet, pathetically, I'm still hesitating.

What if, like poor Rapunzel's father, I get caught creeping over the wall at dead of night? What if my mysteriously invisible neighbours, with their mysteriously immaculate garden and maliciously planted trees, turn out to be nothing less than a coven of witches? Highly unlikely, you may think. But this is the West Country, after all – famously prone to the black art. And there is certainly *something* unsavoury about the goings-on next door.

With only half-hearted apologies to the tree lovers, I admit I've just now looked up 'tree murder' on the internet, in search of an even simpler, less traceable killing method; one which won't involve my stepping into the witches' garden at any point. Sadly I found nothing very helpful except a news report about a man in the Midlands, jailed for poisoning his neighbour's leylandii by peeing on it every night. If even peeing is imprisonable these days, I'm guessing a tree-crime involving sharp objects will land me straight in Guantanamo Bay.

I could risk the jail sentence, of course. I could … pretend to consider that option.

Or I could try a more conventional approach. Introduce myself to the mysterious witch-neighbours and invite them over to enjoy our view while they still can: try to charm them into compliance. On consideration, I think that may be the way forward.

So the current plan (always subject to changes, of course) is to track down my son's Spiderman football, wherever it may be, and then to throw it over the wall into their garden. It will give me an excuse to go over and introduce myself. I tried to introduce myself before, but they refused to come to the door. This time, with Spiderman and the tree issue spurring me on, there'll be no getting rid of me.

And if - by some glorious chance - a green-faced old crone in a dark pointy hat does happen to answer the door, at least two of my problems will be solved. It'll give me something meaty to talk about not just this evening but for many evenings to come. (Because witches beat movie stars any day.) And the husband will be back so fast to buy up the film rights, he'll have plenty of time to cook the children's din-dins himself.

March 14th

It snowed last night. When we woke up this morning the hills were completely covered and the sky was a deep, clear blue. It was – is – staggeringly beautiful. The children were beside themselves with excitement, of course, and I think I was almost as excited as they were. I cooked them microwave porridge for breakfast, which was meant to be a treat (needless to say they both turned their noses up at it) and, for the first time since we moved here, I succeeded in getting them both ready for school with enough time to spare, or so I thought, for us to walk there. It's further than I realised, actually. It took us over two hours, door to door. We arrived sodden, and very, very late, but appropriately rosy-cheeked. Actually it was wonderful. We cut across the back field, covered in a thick blanket of untrodden snow, and we had to leap from stone to stone to get across the stream. The children looked so happy – and so *old fashioned*. For a moment I remembered why we had wanted to move to the country in the first place.

Fin says he can't make it home this weekend, for reasons which sound annoyingly plausible. He seems pretty unhappy about it, and he claims he's coming home for four nights in a row next week, *en route* to somewhere else. I can't even remember where.

Was he always away as much as this? He says he was. He claims that in London, where I had my own life and my own friends, I just didn't notice it so much. But it's not true. Because at least half the time he's away now he's away *in London*, which means – had we still been in London, he wouldn't actually be away at all.

The children miss him a lot. If he and I didn't argue so much whenever we saw each other, I suppose I'd miss him too. But something's happened to the balance between us. The truth is, I feel somehow belittled by his endless *business*, as if my life – and the children's – were forever on hold for his.

How I loathe to fall into any middle-aged cliché, and may death by firing squad save me from becoming the sort of drippy, whining *frau* who demands a husband at her side, only so he can drown in fearfulness and boredom alongside her. Anyway. Bugger it. How stupid is all this?

He's busy. He has a life.

Clearly it's time I found some business of my own.

Finally talked to Hatty. It was very tense. She called me. As soon as I picked up she said, 'Oh. So you're not dead then,' and the conversation grew increasingly less enjoyable from there.

I said congratulations on the Oscar, and made a chippy, not remotely amusing 'joke' about her conquering the film industry even more efficiently than Fin. Which was a cue, or so she interpreted, for her to launch into a long spiel about Fin's general *fantasticness*, which speech I certainly could have done without, and which I sat through with teeth so tightly clamped it actually gave me a headache.

She also said she hadn't seen or spoken to Damian, and that he's made no attempt to contact her or the children since she threw him out. She said it was a relief for all of them to have his lugubrious presence out of the house at last. So. I said something about how kind she was to be having Fin to stay so often, and very nearly gagged as I said it.

And then suddenly she announced her boss was calling her over. I didn't think she even had a boss.

And we said goodbye. And that was it.

I feel horrible. Not sure if I was the complete bitch or if she was. Keep fighting the urge to call her back and apologise. But how can I? She and Finley would probably open a bottle of champagne in bed together tonight and have a bloody good laugh about it.

Or maybe I'm imagining the whole thing.

Friday March 18th

It's been over a week – more like two – since I last heard anything from Darrell, and now that he's gone silent I'm beginning to think it was pretty pathetic of me not to have returned his text messages in the first place. It's not like he's asked me elope with him, for God's sake. He's only asked me for a game of tennis. Unfortunately.

Joke.

Anyway I've decided I'm going to call him. Maybe he'll call me first. I know he takes Friday afternoons off. And if he doesn't, I'm going to text him first thing Monday morning.

Ha! I was heading out to Waitrose this happy Friday afternoon, when who should come loping up the garden path towards me but ... Darrell. Enjoying his afternoon off.

By sheer, sheer chance I happened to have spent a lot of time in front of the mirror this morning. Don't know why. With the book cruelly overdue now, and me screening all calls to avoid Editor and Agent, I've taken to putting a coat on over my pyjamas to drop off children at school, and not usually bothering to get dressed until it's time to pick them up again. On this occasion, however, by sheer chance, I was wearing earrings and eyeliner and some quite uncomfortable high-heeled boots. Also, some of Dora's peppermint-flavoured lipgloss. Clare Gower would have been impressed. I think Darrell was. He whistled.

Yes he did.

I almost wish our meeting had ended just there. Well, no, I don't. In any case the Waitrose trip was abandoned, which means there is no food in the house. And – this not being Shepherds Bush – no shops open to buy any. Looks like Shreddies for supper again.

More interestingly, though, there was, we felt, a hint of sunlight behind the damp sky this afternoon, so Darrell

and I sat out on the steps of our newly paved, unbelievably bumpy front terrace, and drank coffee, and talked.
About a lot of things actually: Hatty and her short film;
the escalating spat between him and Potato Head
(Potato's been ripping him off for months, apparently);
but mostly about my neighbours and their poplar trees.
He laughed when I suggested they might be witches –
said, intriguingly, that it wasn't the first time anyone had
suggested it. I couldn't tell if he was joking and he would-
n't be drawn. All he would say was that he and Potato
Head had done some work for them a few years ago, and
that they had both agreed they would never do it again.

Apparently there's a husband and wife in the house,
and there also used to be a couple of miserable, pasty-
faced teenagers, but nobody's seen either of them for
years. Which means they must have left home, lucky
things … or, as Darrell suggested, before releasing a laugh
that might have been heard across the entire county,
they've been slaughtered and added to the parents' caul-
dron.

'Witchcraft's the least of it, from what I hear,' Darrell
said. 'You'd be surprised what's supposed to go on in that
house.'

I begged him to tell, but he just shook his head and
laughed his incredibly sexy laugh, and warned me to be
careful, because *even if I couldn't see them, they were watching me*. What did he mean? Darrell always looks a little
like he has his own private joke going, and it was pretty
much impossible to tell whether he was teasing. My mind
has been running wild on the possibilities ever since.

Anyway, we finished our coffee and headed back down the hill together, me to go and pick up my children from their posh little private school in Paradise; Darrell to visit his four-year-old son, Daniel, who lives with Denise (Darrell's ex-girlfriend) and Denise's mother, Sue, who has emphysema and lives in a wheelchair, and Denise's boyfriend, Mark, who is unemployed, and Mark's brother, Stevey, who is a bit simple (but who, like Mark, sometimes moonlights for Darrell), and Denise and Mark's twin baby daughters, Daisy and Emily, who are apparently both pretty cute. They live, the seven of them, in a bungalow built by Darrell and Mark together, in a big village about three miles on the other side of Paradise. Darrell usually eats with son and family about three nights a week.

But not tomorrow night, I think. Because Darrell and I have made a plan to play tennis together again! We're meeting at the tennis club in Paradise at half past five, which is fine because the courts have floodlights.

Darrell offered to swing by and pick me up, but I said no. Not sure why.

It may not happen anyway. Everything depends on the babysitter and I haven't spoken to her for months. She may well be busy, it being a Saturday night. In fact, for all I know she could be dead.

Bloody well hope not.

Saturday
Very late
Very very very late

Can't sleep. Don't think I'll ever be able to sleep again. Got back at two, and little Ripley had already crept into my empty bed. He's lying beside me now, snoring very gently, and I'm absolutely lashed and absolutely *not* tired, and I'm fighting the urge to wake him up and smother his sweet round innocent cheeks with disgusting alcoholic kisses and to tell him that *it's all going to be all right*; that I love him more than my life, more than *my life*, and that whatever happens – *whatever happens* – he and Dora … Where was I? What am I saying? Can't remember. God, I'm pissed. Stoned, actually, too. Darrell rolls a fine spliff, I think. Among other things. Oh, fuck.

But it was a great evening. It was. Also … very, very difficult, talking to the babysitter without smirking. Wonder if she noticed? She looked kind of sour. Perhaps. Actually maybe she looked exhausted.

I'm so tired. I can't sleep.

It's been a long, long day.

Sunday

Very very very early

It's already light outside and I still haven't slept a wink. The children are going to be awake any minute, and I've got to write some stuff down before then because my thoughts are … not under any kind of control, and I need to get a few things straight.

It was a good evening. We didn't play tennis for long – there wasn't any point. I mean it was stupid, we both knew. Even at the beginning he was pausing between serves to ask me if I supported the war, for Heaven's sake. (*He does*, weirdly. But his best friend is serving in Iraq at the moment, so maybe that has something to do with it.) In any case, we went through the motions, and even with his mind on the Iraq War he played like a god, really, with effortless, faultless grace – and I have to say, there's something about a man who plays truly beautiful, elegant tennis. It's very rare. Actually Fin does. He plays almost as well as Darrell. But not quite as well. Anyway I'm not thinking about Fin at the moment. Don't want to think about Fin …

Where was I? Darrell just kept blocking my shots back at me, and laughing, and however hard I hit the ball, however slyly I thought I angled it, it just came bouncing back –

   & back

   & back

   & back

Until I was almost dead with the effort to win a single honest point off him, and Darrell was laughing so hard that I couldn't really help laughing too, in spite of feeling quite stupid. The set degenerated pretty much from there. We played the last few games with me cheating blatantly, and Darrell just laughing, and lobbing the balls back, and asking disconcerting questions in the middle of seemingly endless points.

'Did your mum go bonkers, then. Before she copped it?' was one.

'Do you believe in life after you die?' was another

'What would you do if your son said he wanted to be policeman?'

'Have you ever done it with two men at the same time?' Cheeky sod. That was when we gave up on the tennis and went to the pub instead.

Same pub, same table by the fire. It was still early – only about half past six – but the place was already lively. We were there for an hour or so, until a party of rugby players came in and Darrell mentioned he had some spliff in the van. We were going to smoke it outside. That was the original plan. But it was cold. Cold-ish. And anyway it turned out he'd left the spliff at home, not in the van, he said, and since his flat was only five minutes away we were pretty much already there anyway. So we got into the van and he drove us back to his flat, above the Oxfam shop, just behind Paradise High Street.

The flat was small and messy and not that nice, but it didn't matter much. He made some toast, which neither of us ate, and he opened a couple of cans of beer and we sat side by side on his sofa, and he rolled a nice, big fat joint. We smoked it together, and talked, and giggled a bit, and I felt a bit like I was twenty again, but in a good way. Twenty, but better. Our legs were touching, but it didn't matter. I mean to say – it was obvious. It was inevitable. And it's been so long, now, I've been off the shelf, out of circulation, or whatever. But the funny thing is it felt completely natural. He kissed me, as I knew he would. And it was better, even, than I had ever thought it would be. I stayed for a long time after that.

He went out at some point, fetched more tobacco and alcohol, and some liquorice allsorts, I remember. I dozed, briefly. (Didn't much want to think.) And then he came back. I stayed for a bit longer. I took a shower. He drove me back to the tennis club, where my car was still waiting for me. And then I drove here, home, to the Dream House; to the genteel, whispery babysitter, whom I felt could see straight through into my cheating soul.

And, finally, to my own bed. And a total inability to sleep.

It was a good evening, though. Better than good. Much, much better. And I don't feel guilty. Why should I? This is my life. My business. Fin's never around anyway. It has nothing to do with him.

Darrell and I didn't talk about a Next Time. I don't

know, yet, if I want one. Or even if he does, come to that. I mean I do. God, I do. But I – the – *fuck*! What do I know? Guilt. Confusion. Guilt. God, I just don't know anything any more.

Ripley's waking up. Better pull myself together. I've promised to take them to the cinema today – if there's anything showing, that is, and if all the tickets haven't already been booked up. Bloody Hell. I never imagined there would come a day when I would actually feel nostalgic for Leicester Square. Any case. And here comes Dora. Got to go.

Tuesday

Fin's due back tomorrow. I'm having a drink with Darrell tonight. Part of me wants to cancel him. In fact most of me wants to cancel him, because I've been thinking about him solidly since Saturday night, and my skin – everything – my mind, my body's all on fire. Like a bloody teenager. I can't concentrate. I can't work. I can't eat. I can't sit still. I can't do anything. It's a nightmare. And honestly I don't know if I can trust myself to be able to keep this – whatever it is – under any kind of control. I need to pause; spend these four days with Fin, and try to work out what the hell's going on between us. Got to try and make some sense out of things.

Wednesday

I called Darrell and the babysitter about five o'clock yesterday afternoon and cancelled them both. Told Darrell the babysitter was sick. He suggested sending his sister Denise over, but I said no, and he seemed to take that OK. I thought it was the end of the matter. But then he called back half an hour later, sounding ... angry, I suppose, and maybe even a bit wounded. He'd rung a woman friend who did babysitting, to see if she could help me out. She'd been delighted. She said she'd been due to babysit that evening anyway, except the mother had just rung up and cancelled her ...

He said to me: 'If you didn't want to see me, why didn't you just say so? I feel like a pillock now.'

I said I didn't know, I was sorry, that I did want to see him, which I do, but that I needed a bit of time to think – and without another word he put the phone down. I badly wanted to call him back, but I didn't. Because I suppose I realised, maybe a little later than he did, that there wasn't really much point. We had nothing more to say to each other. At least for now.

Fin's due in on the late train tonight. Just spoken to him. He sounded very tetchy. I get the impression he's looking forward to our next few days together almost as much I am. At least – that's unfair. He's desperate to see the children, and the children are so excited about seeing him they can hardly stand up straight. They spent the whole weekend making a 'WELCOME HOME' banner for him, and they're up on the landing at the moment, trying to attach the wretched thing to the banisters. In fact it sounds like Ripley's got stuck. I think I'd better go and help him.

COUNTRY MOLE

Sunday Times

—————◆————

Sex, sex, sex. That's all I can think about this week, reader! It's been quite a lively time down here in Paradise. And I think I've finally made a friend! He and I met up for our second game of tennis on Friday. And guess what? *We ended up in bed!* Except – ha, of course, when I say *bed* I mean pretty much anywhere but. A bed. I mean –

To the dirty details, then. Every filthy one of them! Darrell (that's the non-biscuit-eating builder to you – that's right, the man who built our beautiful kitchen), *my friend Darrell* … has a body like – Or, no, I won't even begin on the body, yet. He has hands like a – He does things with his hands like a –

Like a –

Ohhh, fuck it.
Fuck it.
Fuck fuck fuck.
I need a cold shower. I need an icy cold bath. I need a – Ah! And here comes the postman to bring me back to earth. To bore me into a stupor. To talk about bloody

trees, and maybe calm me down a bit … Hello post-man. What have you got for me today? Have you got a man with hands like a –

Right then. Start again. *Start again.*

… Or maybe not, actually. This is never going to work. Column's not due in until tomorrow, anyway. I'll do it this evening. Be a good excuse to avoid having to deal with Fin.

Friday

Start again. To business. And now I've got that horrible letter, I can write about Darrell without mentioning his –

Deep, deep breath.

And start again.

COUNTRY MOLE

Sunday Times

———◆◆◆———

Heartbreak and chaos all round down here in Paradise. The husband's abroad and has been (on and off) for some time. The landscape gardener has wasted our money and moved on, the dog's on heat and been missing since seven o'clock this morning, the ceiling has collapsed onto our state-of-the-art new kitchen, and – worst of all – the handsome man who built it, who used to sing Fred Astaire songs while he worked, has just sent us a bill out of the blue complaining of 'unforeseen labour and expenses', and demanding an extra £1,400. I don't know what he's playing at.

So far I've ignored the bill. I've put it in various places, on mantelpieces and bookshelves and different desks and am happy to report that I've now lost it completely. But I'll have to confront the thing eventually. The man's not-so-handsome partner has already started texting me, which is slightly unnerving.

More than unnerving, actually; slightly depressing – because as it happens the other one (the handsome one) and I played tennis a couple of times not so long ago. We drank cider together afterwards and everything. I think I thought he was a friend.

Ditto the landscape gardener. She seemed lovely at the beginning: woolly and vague and full of earthy, West Country humour. She was meant to be levelling the delicate slope on our front terrace and, because she said she was a missionary's daughter, I agreed to pay her in advance. Somehow she's managed to transform what was once a faintly annoying tilt into something resembling the Matterhorn; so steep and bumpy the children have been using it for tobogganing.

When I suggested, tentatively, that the terrace could perhaps have been made a fraction flatter, the woolly missionary's daughter's voice soared in rage. Her character transformed. 'There's only so flat you can get a place,' she screamed. I didn't know what to say to that, so I offered her goat's cheese soup from the microwave and apologised profusely. It seemed to calm her down. Her voice returned to normal. And then she wandered away, leaving sacks of sand and cement scattered about the garden. I haven't seen her since.

The kitchen ceiling, meanwhile, collapsed about a fortnight ago, maybe even longer - because I left the upstairs bath running one day while I took the children to school. We thought we'd found a builder to fix it. Or rather, the husband did. He tracked somebody down via the net - not only that, somebody who claimed he could start immediately, which was clearly a point in his favour. We had decided to overlook the fact that he came without a landline, a physical address or even any references, because we were desperate. We still are. Or the husband is. I've got pretty used to it, to be honest.

In any case the builder came round on Friday, three days before work was due to begin. The husband, who was meant to have been there to meet him, had needed to rush off back to London at the last minute. So. It was just me and the builder. He seemed to be very nice; very reassuring. But half an hour after leaving he called my mobile and declared he couldn't, after all, do the job without a £3,000 advance. In cash. Obviously I tried to barter him down. Might he, I wondered, possibly be able to manage with slightly less? £1,000, for example. It didn't go down so well. He announced it was impossible for him to work when there was an 'issue of trust' between us, and he hung up, and oddly enough he's been screening mine and the husband's calls ever since.

... Still no sign of the dog by the way. Nearly six hours she's been gone now. I'm wondering whether I can get her a morning-after pill - that is, if she ever comes back again. Our local vet is strictly homeopathic so I don't suppose he'll approve, but something's going to have to be done. There's a disgusting, mangy old sheepdog taken to camping on our new, perpendicular terrace. And it's impossible, through so many layers of dangling sheep-shit, to make out its gender either way, but his sudden affection for our doorstep makes me fear the worst.

Of course there comes a moment, at times like these, when painful questions have to be asked. For example, can I really remain blameless amid this litany of unfortunate events? Or is there something about me, something flash and metropolitan which a) prevents me from switching off baths and closing doors behind animals on heat, and b) beams like a magnet across the West Country, attracting crooks to my Prada-imitation wallet – Oh goodness, but here comes the dog! Walking a bit funny. Better get off to the vet.

Thursday April 12th

Fin's home again. He's been home solidly for six days now and he intends to remain here until at least the weekend, possibly even until Tuesday. I suppose I ought to be pleased, but he's been pacing around the house like a caged animal, all knotted up with irritation because of the supposed chaos. I don't even notice it any more. If I ever did. In fact he's been in a sort of perma-frott of disapproval pretty much the entire week and it's got to the point now where I think I can hear his tongue clicking from the bloody village shop. I'm beginning to long for him to go away again. At least then I'd be able to watch telly in bed.

He was meant to have gone back to London two days ago but for some mysterious reason he decided against it. He says he's cancelled a bunch of meetings because, he says, he's fed up with being away from his family – but I don't think I believe him. Apart from the fact that he seems amazingly fed up at being *with* his family, I talked to Hatt's nanny last night (didn't leave a message). She told me Hatt's away in Düsseldorf until Monday. Rotterdam, maybe. Don't care. In any case – quite a coincidence, I don't think. He says Hatt's offered to rent him a room permanently in her big, fat Notting Hill house with ceilings. She didn't even discuss it with me first, the silly cow. And he's going to take her up on the offer. Says it's much more comfortable than the sofabed, and I'm sure it is. I'm sure it is. In the meantime, when he's not ostentatiously tidying neglected corners of this house, he's on the telephone in search of a builder. I get the impression he's not going to give up, either. He's not going to stop until this situation is resolved.

I can't work out if my uncharacteristically Zen-like approach to said catastrophe is in fact nothing more than an elaborate new way of annoying him. A bit worried it may be. Either way, it's a shame I can't extend the Zen feel beyond our damaged kitchen, to our damaged marriage. Fin and I can't seem to look at each other without finding something petty to squabble about. It's horrible. Really, it is. Because I love him. I mean I do. Usually. But he's endlessly *rearranging* things which were perfectly OK in the first place; and always with this sodding great Ready Brek glow of reproach beaming off him. Anyway. Anyway. Maybe it's not easy for him either. Or something. Maybe it isn't. Or maybe he just wishes he was already installed at Hatty's, where there's somebody paid to keep the house looking spotless all the time, and where kitchen ceilings would never be so frivolous as to fall in.

Plus, of course, I still haven't had a chance to speak to Darrell. Not about anything, least of all ... Oh God. Here comes Herr Himmler, demanding to know where I left the secateurs. I've never touched them in my life. I don't think.

Better hide.

Sunday April 15th

Drinkipoos *chez* Clare Gower and her husband last night. Henceforth to be known, I think, as Beauty-Secrets and the Beast. Or possibly not. Bit mean. Mr and Mrs Mega-Bux, perhaps. The Mister is a pretty good Monster – though, it has to be said, a very rich and very helpful one. He's sending his builders round first thing tomorrow to sort out our ceiling. It should all be finished within a couple of weeks.

Fin came with me to the Gowers', too, which made a nice change. It did. We haven't been out together for weeks.

The evening started very badly, though, because it turned out I'd got the wrong date and the drinks party had been and gone the previous evening. How could I have been so stupid? It's the only party we've been invited to in months. Actually it's the only party we've been invited to since we've been down here. And I messed it up.

So – not very surprisingly – the Gower house, beautiful and shiny, was completely silent when we arrived. There were only two cars parked out front (a BMW tank, which Clare drives, and a black sports car, make forgotten but which Fin said was very smart). Nevertheless Fin and I presented ourselves at the front door, all togged up in our drinkipoos finest. We were squabbling with each other, in whispers, about whose fault it was that we had obviously arrived either too early or too late – and then Clare appeared. She was nibbling on a pomegranate and wearing a silky, peachy négligé with skimpy, coordinating dressing gown on top. It could, feasibly, have been a party outfit, I thought. I hoped. But then I noticed the look of astonishment on her face, and the fact that she was also wearing furry slippers.

She gazed at the two of us in silence. I said, 'Oh God. It's the wrong night, isn't it?' And she just burst out laughing. She was lovely – just as she had been the last time, when I forgot she was coming to lunch. She ushered us both in, despite our protests. And we did protest a lot – the poor woman was dressed for bed … But she was adamant that we stayed. In fact she more or less pulled Fin into the house. 'Better late than never!' she cried. 'I was only vegging in front of the telly, anyway! Come on in! Roger's here! I'll pop upstairs and get changed and then we can all have a lovely lovely drink!' It occurred to me vaguely that she might have had one or two lovely ones already. She was a bit clumsy, in her furry slippers, and a tiny bit red in the face. 'Honestly, girl,' she said to me, 'you'll be forgetting your own head next!'

We followed her through the newly refurbished hall to the sitting room, also newly refurbished, as she was quick to point out. 'Completely different,' she exclaimed, 'since our little coffee morning! Don't you think?' I'm not certain I would have noticed. It looked pretty much completely the same to me. Well, maybe very slightly more luxurious – from a club-class airport lounge to a first-class, sort of thing; but the beiges and oatmeals all seemed to be unchanged.

'It looks amazing,' I said cleverly. Which it did, in fact, if you rate sheer luxury before any semblance of individual taste. And after an evening of cosseting in that sitting room, I sincerely wish more people did. Anyway, Clare was very pleased with the sitting room's new look. She explained to Fin, who gave every appearance of being riveted, that the room had been so mucky before, she'd been forced to start completely from scratch: fresh carpets, new sofas, new curtains – even the paintings had been bought in. The room smelled of lilies, which was nice; and when Clare fixed us our drinks from the bar at the back of the room I noticed she used a little machine which frosted our glasses with a fine sheen of ice. Thrilling.

Before she disappeared upstairs to change she poured Fin a perfectly frosted tumbler of whisky and then delivered it to him, in all her peachy finery, swaying and purring just like Jessica Rabbit. 'So, *Mr Film Producer,*' she said to him, 'we meet at last! I can't believe it's taken so long. I've heard so much about you ...'

I remember at school there used to be girls who completely transformed as soon as there were boys in the room. She was like that. It was definitely embarrassing, I thought. Fin, I have to say, didn't seem to mind in the least.

She disappeared for half an hour after that, returning in cream-coloured woollen trousers, cream-coloured high heels and a silk cream blouse, and carrying a plateful of smoked salmon and cream cheese sandwiches. By then her husband had already joined us.

He'd sauntered in a couple of minutes earlier, looking small and, understandably enough, quite bad tempered. I apologised for barging in on his evening, but he brushed it aside with a flick of his pudgy, Mega-Buck wrist. 'Not at all. Not at all,' he said, without really looking at me, and made himself a frosted gin and tonic. Or frosted gin, actually, mostly. In any case. Then he plonked himself down on a big, fat, creamy sofa and addressed himself to Fin.

'You fixed your ceiling yet?' he said. Like black treacle, his voice was: deep and arrogant and unhealthy, full of phony poshness and pure corruption. It might have been quite sexy, in fact, if its owner hadn't been so small.

In any case, before Fin had even started to shake his head, Mr Mega-Bux (Roger) had already flashed out his mobile telephone. He was already speed-dialling what I assumed was his PA.

'Yaahh. Liza darling. I need you to call O'Connor for mé. Could you tell him Mr Gower needs a favah. Got a job for him. *Great, great* friend of ours urgentlé needs a ceiling put in. Yup, pronto. Could you organise that? Liza, you're an angel. You're a star. Thank you, darling. Just tell his girl to call my wife, would you?' At which point his wife appeared before him, offering up her sandwich plate. He took one sandwich – beautiful, delicate, perfect little sandwich that it was – and shovelled it into his mouth without glancing at it or her. 'Clare'll have all the details,' he said, munching through. And he hung up. Turned to the wife. Wrinkled his nose in dissatisfaction. 'Do we have anything more cheesé?' he asked. She tripped off to the kitchen to find out.

'So.' Roger said, looking at Fin. 'Clare tells me you're in films. Ever come across Sharon Stone? I tell you, that's one lady I'd definitely pay some change to know better.' And they were off. Sharon Stone. Sale and Leaseback. Sharon Stone ... tax breaks ... investment opportunities ... Sharon Stone. Heaven.

Clare, when she wasn't hopping up and down in search of cheesy things for her husband, and when she wasn't offering sandwiches and cleavages to mine, very sweetly invited Ripley and Dora round next week to go riding. We're going on Wednesday, as soon as the school breaks up.

Something funny happened when I talked about our neighbours and the poplar trees. Roger Mega-Bux listened to the story with half an ear, and immediately announced we should sue, though he was unwilling to be specific on what grounds. 'It doesn't matter what grounds,' he said dismissively. 'Get your solicitor to send them one of his nasties. Those trees'll be sawdust by breakfast, I'm telling you.' He shovelled something cheesy into his mouth, and in the slightly long pause, while we all waited for him to swallow, Clare Gower said, 'Roger's got a point, you know. Don't you think, Fin?'

'Who are they, these bloody fools?' Roger demanded (talking over her, as it happens). 'Do we know them, Clare?'

Clare didn't answer. She asked Fin if his drink was all right.

I said I didn't know their names, but that I thought Clare did, and I asked her and she said, 'Oh, goodness, I can't even remember now.' At which point it was pretty obvious something was wrong.

'What are they called, Clare?' Roger asked again.

She said, 'I think they're called – oh gosh, I really can't remember. Hunter- Somethingorother, I should think. I honestly can't remember, Roger. Does anyone want another drink?'

'Ah. Mr and Mrs Hunter-Robinson,' said Roger, looking straight at her. 'We know them, don't we, Clare?'

At which point an appalling silence fell – broken, I'm proud to say, by *moi*, thinking on my feet as ever. I asked Clare if she'd mind showing me the way to the lavatory. Which she did.

But what the Hell was all that about?

April 16th

I was coming back from finally introducing myself to one of the unspeakable, mysterious Hunter-Horribles next door, and there was Darrell just in front of me, heading up to the house. I saw him on the path and stopped him before he got any further. Fin was still at home at that point. Not that he could possibly have seen anything. Anyway, I don't want to think about that. Fin's gone now, back to Hatty's house. I don't want to think about him.

It was a beautiful evening. I spotted Darrell strolling carelessly through the long golden shadows, and my heart missed a beat. Unfortunately. He looked thoughtful. Light. Most of all he just looked incredibly, incredibly attractive. He smiled when he spotted me. It was the first time we'd seen each other – the first time we'd had any contact since he hung up on me that time. Still, I didn't smile back. I beckoned for him to come away from the house, and together we snuck out, back onto the village road, onto the bridleway that runs up behind the church, and into the woods.

After a few minutes, when we still hadn't really spoken – except I think I'd apologised for not having been in touch – he sort of pulled me away from the path, and he kissed me. I felt suddenly very angry. Partly, I suppose, because I was terrified – of being caught, or of not being caught, and of everything slipping out of control. Partly because of my own treachery, I think. And partly, to be honest, because of this ridiculous, completely spurious bill he sent us for the bloody kitchen. So – he tried to kiss me; or maybe he did kiss me for a second or two. And instead of behaving with any tiny semblance of dignity, I threw myself backwards, half stumbled into whatever bush it was that was meant to be hiding us, and spat at him to *Piss off*.

He looked pretty shocked by that; not terribly impressed, I think. He stepped away from me; raised his two hands in semi-humorous surrender. 'Fair enough,' he said.

We talked about the bill he'd sent, which – obviously – I haven't mentioned to Fin. And he said he knew nothing about it. Seeing the look of annoyance crossing his face when I told him, it would have been absurd not to believe him. He told me to ignore the wretched bill; to rip it up and forget all about it. He said he'd talk to Potato Head in the morning.

And after that … I suppose I was relieved, maybe. I don't know. But there we were in the woods, on that beautiful, beautiful evening, and we were friends again. Alone. And … Fin was back in the house, packing to go back to his 'room' at Hatt's … and it was all just so … *good*. It was good. It was good it was good it was good.

I told him not to come visiting again. That this must never, ever, ever happen again. Ever. Was he listening? I don't know. Did I mean it? I think so …

I feel sick. I feel permanently bloody sick these days. Guilt, perhaps. Or nerves. Or a mixture of both. What the hell do I think I am doing?

Fin's gone now, anyway. He left a couple of hours ago. Kissed the children goodnight and took a taxi to the train and then another taxi from the train on to Hatt's place. He said he'd be back again at the weekend, and it's only four days until then. But I feel so lonely suddenly. I just wish – everything. Nothing. I don't know. I just wish he'd stop going away.

Friday

Help!!! Just got a call from the *Sunday Times*. I was meant to file yesterday and I forgot. I *forgot!* How pathetic, how completely bloody *useless* is that? I've been writing for fifteen years on and off – probably even more, actually, if I could be bothered to count – and I've *never* just 'forgotten' to deliver my copy before. Never. What's the matter with me? What's happening to me? Now I've only got until lunchtime to file something and I feel so bloody ill I think I'm going to have to write it from bed.

At least I know exactly what I'm going to write about this time. For once. That's what's so ridiculous. I've been thinking about it a lot! How could I just *forget*? Anyway, here goes.

Here goes.

Here goes …

I hope it doesn't sound too crazy when I put it down on paper. Fin said I was barking when I told him. But then of course he would. Men always say women are barking when they're too bloody lazy to try to understand the point.

COUNTRY MOLE

Sunday Times

My mysteriously invisible neighbour, of poplar sapling fame, didn't answer her front door in the traditional witch's garb I had psyched myself into expecting. It was strangely disappointing.

In fact, at first glance, standing there on her porch without her pointy hat on, she looked like any one of the hundreds of forty-something lady-mummies in the area: nice clean hair cut to sensible below-the-ear length; freshly laundered jeans; nice burgundy sweatshirt with rugby logo atop; and a husband nowhere to be seen (in London no doubt, like the rest of them, grubbing up the mortgage for Paradise. Among other things).

She might even have fooled me completely, but last Saturday night she and her husband came to dinner. And I now feel confident to state, more or less categorically (since there's no one to contradict me except my own husband, whose opinion is meaningless anyway because he spent the entire evening on his mobile discussing sale-and-leasebacks with a man in Los Angeles): this neighbour of ours is no ordinary lady-mummy. Pointy hat or no, I'm convinced she has evil powers.

She didn't want to come to dinner. That much was obvious. She didn't want to talk to me at all; didn't want to answer the door, didn't really even want to give me back the football – which was wrecked, by the way: I'd only tossed it over her garden wall a few hours earlier. Now it was flat as pancake. It was covered in teeth marks, and ripped to shreds. Nevertheless I was willing to overlook that. The husband and I didn't leave London to stare into a line of poplar trees. However frosty she wanted to be, I was determined to befriend her.

And here's the thing: laugh if you will, but I've been feeling mysteriously sickly ever since. Our new house has taken on a malignant smell, which my husband, when he's not on the telephone, insists is a delightful mixture of new floor paint, new carpet, and the new plaster in the kitchen ceiling.

Well, perhaps – except before that football-wrecking episode, this house smelled perfectly fine to me. Something has happened.

She arrived early, reeking of scent, and with her husband, the poor dupe, trailing in softly behind her. He's a stockbroker, as I had guessed; yet another Paradise clone – a figure so familiar now, I wondered if we'd even met each other before. The gentlemen in this expensive little corner seem to be peculiarly, extraordinarily interchangeable. Unless I'm missing something. I think I must be. In any case, I don't think he uttered a word which wasn't about train timetables all night. So while the holograph husbands burbled quietly, the one to LA about industry tax breaks, the other to himself about punctuality targets, I struggled hard to find common ground with the sorceress. We talked about the weather, which has been damp. We talked about some traffic lights off the ring road, which she thought would benefit from a cleaning. We talked about the local Waitrose moving the place where they store the trolleys. The trouble was, her *parfum*, on top of the other smells, was making me very ill indeed.

'Once you both get settled here,' she declared at some point, sloshing extra wine into her glass, 'you'll discover the social life tends to centre a lot around the rugby club.'

And that was when the room went cold. I realised, once and for all, that I was dealing with a sociopath. A witch-cum-sociopath, who was desperately trying to imitate 'normal'. It was also when I realised I was going to be sick.

She smiled at me. 'Are you OK?' she asked, leaning forward. 'You look *terrible*. You look as though you'd much prefer to be in bed.'

I left the room to throw up. Came back ten minutes later still feeling like death. 'Are you sure you're OK?' she asked again, pouring herself another glass of wine. 'Perhaps we should leave you in peace?' But she and the Dupe didn't do that until 2 a.m. And in all that time those poplar trees never got mentioned. Over and over, the words would form on my lips, only for another of her chillingly 'normal' conversations

to distract me … And I'm still as sick as a parrot.
Is it simply a coincidence?

Draw your own conclusions.

Thursday

Children broke up for the Easter holidays yesterday. Lovely, having their cheerful voices around, after so much time on my own. Trouble is they're not going to stay cheerful for long if I don't come up with a few ways to entertain them. Their friends all seem to have flown away to far-flung corners. One's gone to Kenya. Another one's gone to Egypt. Another one's gone to the Seychelles. Spoilt brats. Haven't they heard of global warming? Also, why have their annoying parents all got so much money to spare? In the meantime, there's a limit to the number of picnics the three of us can have in the bloody rain.

Fin says he's on the Isle of Man meeting up with film financiers. And maybe he is. Who knows? He says he's going to be there all week. I can't remember the name of his hotel, and his mobile, for some reason, doesn't get a signal anywhere on the island. He's rented a telephone from another network and I know he'll say he gave me the number but I can't find it anywhere. That I've bothered to look. He's left several messages – mid-afternoon, just when he knows we're most likely to be out – but we haven't actually spoken to each other for days. The truth is I'm no longer so sure which of us is trying to avoid the other harder. I just don't know anymore.

Most of all I wish I could stop feeling so bloody ill. I'm sure it's nothing. Absolutely nothing. I'm sure I'll be fine in a day or two. I'm absolutely certain it isn't what I think it might be. How can it be? How can it be – this month of all months? Of course it isn't. I don't even want to think about it actually. All the same, maybe it's time I found a doctor.

Took Ripley and Dora over to Clare Gower's place so they and her children, Joshie and Tanya, could go riding together; also so I could finally get the dirt on my evil neighbours, the Robinson-Horribles. I thought, maybe, if Mr Mega-Bux wasn't around to cramp his wife's style she might have been willing to open up a bit.

Except she wasn't. The children were outside on the trampoline (having done their riding, which was a great success) and Clare was cooking up chocolate muffins for tea. I mentioned, very casually I thought, that the Horribles had come round for dinner the other evening.

'It was quite a night,' I said, when she didn't immediately respond. Not sure what I meant by it exactly, but it didn't matter. Luckily she didn't ask.

She said, 'When I make choccie muffins I always add a weeny bit more cocoa than they recommend. Don't you? It gives you that extra choccie zing, which is so important. Especially for kids.'

'They're quite an intriguing couple,' I said. 'Aren't they, though? Very keen on rugby.'

'… Yesss …'

'I mean, they seem so normal. But

then – I don't know. *Maybe they're not?'*

Clare went purple and I immediately felt like the bitch that I am. Here I was in her lovely luxury kitchen, with my children outside bouncing blissfully on her Olympic-size trampoline, and all I could do was torment her with questions she very obviously did not want to answer. 'Goodness,' she said, plopping choccie muffin mix into choccie muffin cases, 'I hardly know them really! *Hardly*, anyway. Roger doesn't really like them, so – you know …' She looked up. And there was definitely fear in her face. 'You didn't mention me?'

I said no, and she relaxed. But I fully intend to now, when I see them again. If I ever see them again. Annoyingly, they've both gone back to being invisible.

Monday

Darrell hasn't called. As he promised he wouldn't, so that's all right. But he sent me a lovely text yesterday. It just said 'Missing you'. That was all. I've kept it. Maybe I shouldn't, but I have. I'm missing him, too. I'm missing Fin. I'm missing London. I'm missing my life. God, I feel so bloody ill.

The children are downstairs; a bit bored, I think. It's raining outside, and all their friends are still away for the holidays. So I'm going to get off my fat, lazy arse, stop feeling so bloody sorry for myself and take them for a swim.

Coming back from the Leisure Centre, steeling myself for the sickly reek of the wretched house, and who should be standing waiting for me on the front porch but Potato Head. Looking pretty damn mean, I might add. I felt a lurch of real fear. Because the fact is, in spite of Darrell promising to speak to him, he's been texting me regularly about this wretched bill, and in fact yesterday, or possibly the day before, he even sent the bill to me again, only this time by registered post.

Which just goes to show how below speed I must be feeling at the moment. Because I never, ever, *ever* sign for letters unless I'm specifically expecting something. Obviously. Why would I? Why would anyone? In any case, I signed for that letter without even thinking. And there it was, another bill from Potato Head, with another demand for £1,400.

I threw it away, actually. And more or less managed to forget about it until the moment I saw him standing there on my front porch, looking menacing.

I told Ripley and Dora to go round and play in the back garden, and continued up the hill to join him.

'Hello,' I said. Which I thought was pretty poised, under the circs. 'What can I do for you, Mr ...' and I realised, too late, I'd completely forgotten his real name. 'Mr Kitchen-Builder,' I said coyly. Just like Clare Gower would have done. Except of course she would have been in a peach silk négligé at the time. I had chlorine hair from the Leisure Centre, and a pasty face, and the top button of my jeans undone. Anyway, I gave him a sickly smile and for some reason he seemed to like that. He smiled back. Possibly for the first time since I've met him. 'If you've come about the bill I think you need to talk to Darrell,' I said. 'I've already discussed it with him and –'

Potato Head leered, I think. He said, *'I'll bet you have.'*

After that I didn't say another word. I called Darrell on the mobile, told him Potato was with me, hassling me about the bill, and tried to get Potato to take the telephone. He refused. He just – almost from the moment I had Darrell on the line, he just began to slink away. By the time I'd told Darrell that Potato was refusing to speak to him, he was already a quarter way down the hill. Darrell said he was coming over. I told him not to. And then I realised I was pretty much about to burst into tears, so I hung up.

And now I'm fairly certain my life is falling apart. In fact I know it is. I don't need a doctor to tell me what's wrong with me. And what happened between Darrell and me didn't happen. Ever. Definitely, definitely, it didn't happen when it did.

And I have got to be bold about that. And I have seriously, seriously got to talk to Fin.

COUNTRY MOLE

Sunday Times

———❖———

Our neighbourhood witch has reverted to her usual
invisible self, so far as I can tell. But her
wretched poplar saplings, destined to block out our
beautiful view, grow taller and more excruciatingly
visible every day. At least they do to me, who,
between bouts of vomiting, can think of little else.
My husband, so engagingly relaxed about all things
domestic he accidentally referred to his London lodg-
ings as 'home' last weekend, says he thinks I'm being
pathetic. He says the trees won't cause any real
obstruction for at least a decade, maybe more, by
which time who knows where we'll be? Possibly dead,
actually, the way I'm feeling at the moment – the way
I've been feeling ever since the witch came to dinner. I do believe I've been hexed.

In London, getting to see a GP is one of life's
greater irritants, usually involving at least half a
day in a waiting room reading old issues of *Family
Circle*, followed by a 90-second consultation with
the back of the doctor's computer, and a slick brush-
off. I had presumed that the NHS experience would be
similar everywhere, even down here in Paradise –

which is why, since we moved eight months ago, the children and I have muddled through sundry afflictions without bothering to sign up to a surgery, or even to discover where one was. We might have continued that way if it hadn't been for the witch's spell. But this new sickness has become a little debilitating. My poor family thinks I'm going mad.

I have taken some kind of allergic reaction to the smell in our lovely, newly decorated house, to the point that now there is only one room where I can breathe freely. It's a small back bathroom, the only room not yet to have been renovated, and it looks as though I may have to set up camp in there, until either the sickness or the smell goes away.

In the meantime, I finally made contact with the local surgery. I didn't mention the witchcraft, obviously. I told them what I felt they needed to know, and they gave me an appointment at once. At once. Yes, they did.

When I first walked into the surgery I had to check with the front desk that I had come to the right place. The waiting room was virtually empty, there was classical music playing, soft lighting, sofas, and on a dainty wicker side table two copies of this month's *Harper's Bazaar*. I'd brought my laptop so I could work while I was waiting – but there was no wait! No sooner had I sat, I was called in. Astonishing. I'm trying not to be boring about this, and failing, I suspect. But these things need to be celebrated. I reckon that short shift in that beautiful, tidy waiting room ranks among the highest points of my entire life down here in Paradise.

In any case the doctor couldn't help. I told her the problem, and she took on that complacent, faintly sadistic look doctors always wear when you tell them you're, em, pregnant – but fail to mention you've also been hexed.

'It's not as simple as that!' I cried. 'Something's happened! I'm allergic to the new house!'

She suggested I contact our builder, handsome and non-biscuit eating, and also, of course, among the most attractive men in the South West. She thought I could ask him about the materials he used; ask him if he knew of anything that might counteract the stink. A reasonable enough suggestion, I suppose, if a bit of a long shot. Except I imagine, given the current state of our once beautiful relationship, he'll think he sniffs lawyers' writs and run for the caves.

In any case I can't contact him. Not for a long time. Apart from the fact that he – or his partner – thinks we owe him £1,400, which we don't, I look bloody terrible. Last time I saw him I was lean and fit and we were playing tennis. I think I'd prefer to spend the entire pregnancy in the back bathroom obsessing about witchcraft and poplar trees than to let him see me like this.

Monday April 30th

Oh what a tangled web we weave when first we practise to deceive. ... I'm beginning to lose track of the official story line, as delivered to readers of the *Sunday Times*, and it's making me nervous. Also – I was having coffee with a bunch of the mothers yesterday, and there happened to be a father there, too. For some reason. Don't know why. Most unusual. He asked me point blank – and out of nowhere – if I was the person writing the column in the *Sunday Times*, and my mind went dead. I heard my heart beating inside my ears, and I literally could not speak.

'It's quite interesting, actually,' he said. Which was nice. 'I think she's finding it very difficult.'

Finally, I said something. I can't even remember what, but I know my face was numb.

The mothers didn't seem to be listening, luckily. They all looked pretty blank, and I'm fairly certain it passed off OK. But what about next time? Or the time after that? The coffee mothers are the only adults I speak to these days, from one week to the next. Not only that – and sometimes it's so hard to remember this when I'm mid scribbling about them – but they're real people: decent, kind, friendly; nicer than I will ever be. If they somehow learned that I was ... I don't even want to think about it, actually.

Got a crazy letter from a reader last week, advising me to join a church group and to concentrate much harder on the state of my soul. I wondered if she'd somehow guessed about Darrell.

I wish I'd never mentioned him at all now. Not because of Fin. Fin doesn't even realise I'm writing the column – which, in dark, illogical moments, makes me feel extraordinarily bitter and sad, in spite of the fact that he couldn't know, since I've never told him, and he only ever reads the *Observer*.

Anyway, I didn't bother to reply to the reader's letter. Hardly ever do, in fact. Mostly because people who write to newspapers tend to be lunatics, in my experience, and therefore much better left alone. Got a letter from one reader a few years ago, when I was doing a stint on the *Daily Mail*. It said 'WHO THE HELL ARE YOU to comment on a Minister's toilet habits???' But I hadn't. Never. Not once. In any article I had ever written.

Anyway. Where was I? Readers' letters. Readers' wives. God knows.

I'm in the bathroom again. As usual. I've moved my computer in here now. And I'm wishing I'd never mentioned Darrell in the column. I'm wishing I'd never started the column … Christ, I'm wishing all sorts of things.

Tuesday

Fin was pretty good about the baby. He was, actually. God knows, there was so much we didn't say. I broke it to him over the telephone, in the end. Actually I left a message on his mobile. Such is the state of our relationship. Couldn't stand the suspense any longer. I was bloody terrified. Apart from anything else he's always been pretty clear he didn't want any more children.

'Guess what, Fin, turns out I'm pregnant,' I said. ' Better yet, there's a more than sporting chance that you're the daddy!' Didn't say that, of course. Said I had some urgent news for him. Good news, I hoped, and could he call? I think my voice must have sounded a bit weird, because he guessed, just from that. Called back much faster than usual and made a valiant effort to sound pleased. He made a joke about school fees and about me hurrying up writing the next bestseller. Or maybe I did. Maybe I made that joke. I'm only a week off finishing the novel, as it happens. So –

Fin asked when the baby was due and I said I didn't know. I don't think I do know, actually. I think I've forgotten. It doesn't matter, anyway. What the hell does it matter, exactly when it's due? There are still months and months to go.

May 7th

Darrell called. The children were at school, and I was asleep in the bathroom. I've brought the telephone in here now, also a foam seat, bought for 'sleepovers', which folds out into a child-size … Anyway, Darrell wanted to know if I'd heard anything more from Potato Head. I haven't. So. He asked me how I was, and I said fine. I'm fine. He suggested meeting up again and I said maybe. But we can't, of course. Not now.

Anyway. Fin's back on Friday. It'll be nice. I wish he'd come home.

May 9th

Finished the novel this morning! Great moment. Usually I go out and get pissed with anyone and everyone willing to join me. Trouble is, of course, I can't drink at the moment. Plus I've got no one to get drunk with. Also, I feel so ill I can't really tell if the novel's any good. I certainly remember thinking it was, before all this madness began. But that seems like a lifetime ago now. When did all this madness begin? Or has it not even begun? I don't think so. What the fuck am I talking about?

I think I spend too much time alone.

Thursday May 10th
Very late

Poor little Ripley. Poor darling little Dora. Hard to tell what they make of all this, but they're being so sweet and brave and kind. This evening, after I'd kissed them both goodnight, Dora appeared at the bathroom door with the microwave in her arms. She could hardly see over the top. And her eyes looked so big and round with worry, I know she was trying not to cry. She said, 'We can eat our tea and stuff up here with you tomorrow. And we can eat breakfast. Ripley said he wouldn't mind, either. He's going to help me bring all the breakfast stuff up tomorrow.' I didn't know what to say. I hugged her, and thanked her, and tried to reassure her, and somehow managed not to blub until after she was gone.

I don't deserve her. I don't deserve either of them. Oh God. I'm going to be sick again.

May 11th

More blubbing. It's funny – you think you know yourself. You think of yourself as strong, maybe, and functional. I think I did. And then something comes along. It was the same when Mum was dying. Turned out I wasn't the person I thought I was. In fact I was nothing at all. Nerve ends. It's all I am now. A hideous bundle of spitting, blubbing, puking nerve ends.

I was in the car park at Waitrose this morning, turning over similar happy thoughts, and trying, feebly, to summon the energy to get out of the car. But I couldn't. I just sat in there and blubbed. And blubbed. And blubbed. About everything – Fin, Mum, Hatty, the baby. A friend of mine who topped himself back in the early nineties; a friend of mine whose sister-in-law had a nervous breakdown about the time we were leaving school; the death of Princess Di; the cruelty of bullfighting; the pointlessness of the First World War … It was all getting pretty out of hand, and then I felt somebody's eyes on me and I glanced up; because of all the crying I couldn't quite focus at first, but she was standing right in front of the car, looking directly at me. And I suppose, at that point, I wanted to talk to somebody – to anybody. So I smiled. More or less. And as I smiled I recognised her – or we recognised each other. All at once she scowled, turned and scuttled off.

It was Rachel Healthy-Snax. Running away from me. I sat there for another few minutes, blubbing with renewed fervour. I don't think I have ever felt quite so ill or so lonely in my life.

And then there was a little tap on the window. I almost jumped out my skin.

It was Rachel again. Waving tissues and a packet of Jaffa cakes. In spite of all the vile things I've written about her here, I was never so pleased to see anybody. I could have dropped my pasty, metropolitan head onto her burgundy-fleece-covered shoulder and wept with gratitude.

I managed not to do that. Just. Instead I smiled at her again and opened the car door. She climbed in.

Somehow I found myself telling her all about Fin and Hatty. It was strange because it was the first time I had ever spoken about it to anyone and I hadn't realised quite how much it hurt. Not until it all came juddering out. She was so kind. Just so incredibly kind. She let me go on, blubbering and jabbering, I have no idea for how long.

She told me it had taken her five or six years to settle down to life in the country, which came as a surprise. She always looks so at home. Also, she told me that her own Jeremy Healthy-Snax had had an affair when they first moved to Paradise. I could hardly believe it – and I think she spotted incredulity in my face, because she laughed.

'He doesn't look the sort, I know,' she said. And I quickly said that he did – or, rather, that he didn't – or that maybe there wasn't a sort, and she nodded very calmly.

She said, 'They're *all* shits.' It sounded amazingly shocking.

I asked her if Jeremy's girlfriend had been in London, and she shook her head. I also asked her if the girlfriend had originally been a friend of hers (Rachel's) and she shrugged, and looked quite angry for a minute. She said, 'You have to be careful though, don't you? … It doesn't matter now, anyway. It's in the past. But I must admit I do like to keep a close eye on him. Even in London.' She looked at me. There was a gleam of something in her eyes – possibly a small hint of sadism: 'I've got him calling home a couple of times each night now. Sometimes even more. If he's out to dinner, he has to put me on the line with whoever it is he's dining with. I don't care how difficult it is for him. That's the rule. And he knows, if he doesn't call in, I'll be onto him.'

It shook me a bit, that did. Made me almost feel sorry for Jeremy. In fact, looking back, I think it may even have cheered me up, which is a bit worrying. In any case, after that strange moment of intimacy we broke open the Jaffa cakes and talked about other things. She didn't mention her children or their vegetable intake once. She told me about her days as an accountant in London, and it was pretty clear from the way her face came alive that she had enjoyed it. I asked her if she ever missed it. She said 'sometimes': when it was raining, and the children were at school and Jeremy was away. She said there were times when she wondered … But she didn't say about what. She sounded wistful and terribly lonely, suddenly, and it made me wonder about all the women down here – all the smiling lady-mums, who gave up work to wheel trolleys around Waitrose in Paradise. Perhaps they're all secretly as wretched as each other. Or as wretched as I am. I wonder.

Anyway, Rachel isn't the sort to dwell long on her own wretchedness, I don't think. She changed the conversation pretty quickly, and instead told me two excellent pieces of gossip. First, that the mother of a sad little girl called Delilah, who's in Dora's class, had a boob job on her husband's credit card last year, two days after he walked out on her. (He left her for a travelling masseuse who taught 'relaxation techniques' to City execs at their desks.) Apparently the wound went septic and she had to spend last Christmas in emergency surgery having the implants taken out.

Second, and even more interesting: she told me that Clare Gower had an affair with Mr Robinson-Horrible a few years ago, and that *everyone* (except me) knows about it. Mr Robinson-Loathsome became obsessed and when Clare dumped him he'd started stalking her, calling her thirty times a night, arriving at her doorstep in tears, inundating her with bunches of flowers and so on. There had been one night when the police had apparently been called. Or so Rachel claimed. Before she changed her mind. Suddenly she couldn't remember if it had been Clare or Robinson-Loathsome who'd been the stalker, and whether it was *Mrs* Robinson-Loathsome who'd needed to call the police. At any rate, she was definite that the police had been involved, and that one way or another

Clare Gower had made a tremendous fool of herself.

'I don't like to say too much,' Rachel said, her face all knotted up suddenly. 'But the thing about *Clare* is she has one or two personality problems. A lot of people round here don't like her very much.'

I bumped into Clare about an hour later. She was standing at the fish counter when I finally made it into Waitrose. She was standing, staring blankly at the fish, and I've never seen anyone look so miserable in my life. She transformed in a flash when she saw me. Pinged right back to Perky. And so did I, I suppose. I hadn't seen her for a few days – she said she'd been away visiting her sister – and I was pleased to bump into her. So pleased that I even suggested we had lunch together after we finished shopping. But she said she couldn't. She said the beastly money-maker was at home and waiting to be fed. Poor woman.

COUNTRY MOLE

Sunday Times

———◦◦◦———

I was going to be perfect; a perfect, merry, country mother who only bought food from farmers' markets; who taught her children the difference between mushrooms and toadstools; who filled the house with home-made jam and rescued baby hedgehogs, and clean, wholesome, high-pitched laughter and – oh sugar-and-shoot. It's been nine months we've been living in rural paradise and it's no good pretending things have panned out exactly as I'd envisaged.

The hex upon me continues to gather momentum, and I now retch at the faintest whiff of the inside of our magnificent dream home. Sometimes, if the breeze is right, even the outside makes me want to vomit. Though nobody else seems to notice it, the place reeks of stale fertiliser and rotting metal. And for about a week now, I've surrendered to it. I'm eating, sleeping and working in the back bathroom, out of view of the witch's house next door and presumably, therefore, beyond her hexing power. It's the only room in the house not yet to have been renovated, and it's the only place I can breathe without being sick.

Actually this room stinks too, according to the children: of stale food and grime and rotting lemon peel. I can't notice it, but they're probably right, since my anti-smelling hex makes artificial fragrances of any kind repulsive to me now – soap, shampoo, deodorant, clothes and dishwashing powder included. There was an advertisement on television not long ago, featuring a TV chef whose name I've forgotten. 'Citrus!' he cries, squeezing out a lemon with his bare hand, making it all seem lovely. 'Nature's cleanser!' In desperation, I've bought sacks of the bloody things. I don't know which bit of nature his 'citrus' was supposed to be cleansing, but it's certainly not cleansing anything in Paradise. And now there are lime pips all over the bathroom floor.

My husband, fresh from the Cannes Film Festival, is now on the Isle of Man, shooting a sci-fi film about evil androids overtaking the world. Since it costs almost as much to fly to Douglas as it does to Australia, he'll be stuck there, with the androids and Heaven knows who else, for the next three months. So. That's him gone – and thanking God, no doubt, for exorbitant ticket pricing. He has a foolproof excuse to keep his distance from us, and who can blame him? I'm certainly no fun to be with at the moment. Not that I ever am when I'm pregnant.

Meanwhile the children are stuck with me, poor little devils. We've brought the microwave and a telly into the bathroom, and I keep a little store of food in the shower cubicle. So, once I've fetched them from school they squeeze in here for the evening, one of them in the bath, doing her homework, the other one playing with cars in the dirty laundry basket ...

Oh, but I bet you think I'm exaggerating.

On a more positive note ... Yes ... Shuffled off to another coffee morning yesterday. (Anything to escape the smell.) This one was for charity, I'm proud to announce. There was a cake sale, and a jewellery sale, and a little raffle at the end. I can't honestly remember anything about it, except for one seemingly endless conversation with a Yorkshirewoman who was overflowing with advice about hand lotions.

But I escaped her eventually and headed off with my laptop to the local library. Where a caricature librarian with iron-grey hair and knockers which brushed her kneecaps informed me that plugging in computers was strictly forbidden. It was a health'n'safety issue, she said. Well, of course it would be. Odd, though, because I've been doing it in libraries all over London for years.

But that's Paradise for you in a nutshell. Things are so peaceful down here, any deviation from the norm (in this instance a lot of bored old duffers leafing aimlessly through free copies of the *Daily Telegraph*) and the inmates start to get irritable.

OK. That positive note went a little flat at the end. I'll try again. On a more positive note ... I'm think I'm going to be sick.

I'll be positive next time.

May 18th

Told Fin my decision and he hung up on me. He thinks I'm inventing the problem. Or he says he does. But why would I? Why? Why the hell would I do that?

The sickness is getting worse, even in the bathroom, and for the last couple of nights I've woken up with my stomach heaving, already half way to throwing up. I can't really go on like this. Apart from the fact that I am truly, bloody ill, it's not fair on the children.

Fin won't help. Refuses to get involved. Thinks I'm being hysterical. Well, I feel hysterical. Actually, I've never known him so hard. So completely detatched. It was like talking to a stanger.

I don't even want to think about him anyway. Luckily I've got money stashed for the tax man, also a cheque due in from my publisher any minute. I've already been on to the tourist board. Paradise, needless to say, is overflowing with holiday cottages to let.

We're moving out.

Hatty called this evening. About ten minutes after Fin hung up on me. God, they're pathetic. It's actually the first time she and I have spoken in weeks, and I couldn't help pointing it out. She said, 'I know, God, *sorry*. Just been so busy, catching up with things at work. After all the ridiculous fuss with the Oscar and everything … I know I've been completely useless. Anyway, here I am! Better late than never!'

'If you say so,' I said, but she ignored me. She put on a stupid, phony laugh, which no doubt worked a treat for her in Hollywood, and said, 'Now listen, honeybun.' *Honeybun? HONEYBUN?* The silly cow is fucking my honey-bunny-fucking husband, and she's calling me *honeybun*. 'My spies inform me you've been living in the bathroom the last couple of weeks.'

'That's right.'

'But, sweetie' – and she laughed again – '*why?*'

'Why? Your "spies" didn't tell you I was pregnant, then?'

There was, I think, the minutest pause, and then she said, 'Oh-my-*God*! But that's fantastic!' and I absolutely knew that she already knew. And since I've not mentioned the fact to a soul yet, not even to the poor children, there's only one person who could have told her. 'I have to be honest,' she said. 'I did slightly wonder … Especially when Fin said you were now planning to move out of the bathroom and out of the house altogether. Sweetheart, d'you think you might be being a *teeny* bit crazy? You do go quite crazy when you're pregnant. And it's such a beautiful, lovely house.'

'I'm sick,' I said.

'Well, of course you're sick. Everyone's sick for the first bit.' (Except Hatty, funnily enough.)

I don't know why, but in spite of everything, for a

moment I longed for her to understand; maybe I hoped she would justify it all to Fin; help to get him back on my side, somehow. I feel so bloody lost without him. Maybe, for a moment, I even hoped we could still be friends. I don't know. I don't know. In any case, I tried to explain. And I can still hear how desperate it must have sounded. 'This is nothing like the others, Hatt,' I said. 'I've never known anything like this.'

She said, 'Oh, come on. For God's sake. I've been pregnant. We've all been pregnant before. Fin's beside himself with worry. You've just got to pull yourself together.'

So I hung up. She's tough, Hatty. Always has been. It's one of the reasons we were ever friends. Because so am I – normally. Trouble is it means she doesn't – she can't – put up with people when she senses they're being pathetic. But I am *ill*, for God's sake. Why will nobody believe it?

She's left a couple of messages since, and I think she may even have apologised in one of them, but I am not speaking to her. Not now, nor ever again. Fin, neither. The pair of them can sod off to the Isle of Man, with all her millions, and screw each other senseless for the rest of their senseless lives. God knows what I'll tell the poor children, but nobody else is going to miss them. I certainly won't.

May 20th

Can't get a telephone signal in the holiday cottage. Not that anyone calls, really. Still. Have to take the mobile up the lane every now and then, just in case. And then I get lost. Got lost this morning. All the lanes look the same around here. Can't see over the top of them. And when you can, there are only fields on the other side. Fields and fields and bloody fields. How I hate them.

May 21st

Got a message from my agent. Says she's read the book. Wants to suggest a few changes. Says I have to call.

Absolutely mustn't, though. Absolutely *must not* call. Can't do it. Not fit to talk to anyone at the moment. Least of all reality. I mean a voice from reality. Thank God nobody ever calls me from the *Sunday Times*. I just file, and then there it is in the paper. Mostly. Except when I forget, that is, and the other time last week when she called and I was feeding carrots to the cows, so I didn't want to frighten them. She said, *Good news. John's a big fan*, and I said, *John who? Fan of what?* I'm losing the plot.

Got to pull myself together. Also, it's column-writing day tomorrow. Got to write the column tomorrow. Got to pull myself together. Got to get my head together. Got to do something about my hair. Got to buy some clothes that fit. Got to get a sense of humour. Got to get my head together. Got to *pull myself together*. I'm going to watch *Charlie and the Chocolate Factory* with the children. That will be nice. They'll like that. Plus I think we've got some biscuits. And then tomorrow I'll get up early and I'll spend the morning really getting my head straight, and in the afternoon I'll do the column. It'll be fine. Thank God for the column, really. I'd be lost without it. I've got so much to say to everyone. I think I have. I just wish I knew where to begin.

John who, indeed. Christ. He's only the sodding Editor.

COUNTRY MOLE

Sunday Times

Another bad hair day in Paradise. But things like haircuts aren't so easy to organise any more, involving (as they do) day returns to London and then taxis to and from the hairdresser so as not to miss the cheap train back. Nothing cheap about any of it, of course, and right now I can't afford the expense. The cost of country living just skyrocketed.

We had to evacuate the dream house. Life in the bathroom became pretty much intolerable. So while I'm now paying rent and my husband scrubs about with men-dressed-as-androids on the Isle of Man, desperately trying to cover the mortgage, our beautiful new home stands abandoned. In the last nine months it's been recarpeted, repainted, receilinged, reterraced, refloorboarded, partially extended and partially rebuilt. And now it's empty. It's useless.

Except, I discover, as a source of monumental amusement to some of my old friends back in London. I call them sometimes, hoping for sympathy, and their laughter, on hearing my news, is positively musical. There are times when I have to hold the telephone away from my ear while they recover. In any case I have decided it's not especially helpful to contact any of them, for the time being at least, since when I do we only end up arguing. I seem to have fallen out with everyone.

So the children and I have moved into a studio-style holiday cottage, which backs directly onto a cowpen. It's small - I sleep on the sofa; the children share a bed on the gallery above - but it's larger than the old bathroom and it doesn't stink. Or not of chemicals. As it happens I have always loved the smell of cows and my daughter - oddly - has long nursed an ambition to become a 'cow trainer', though a trainer in what she has yet to decide.

My landlady, the farmer's wife, looks disconcertingly like my London literary agent, I think. Unless I'm hallucinating. So starved of adult company am I that when she came to the door this morning to discuss the broken shower-head (Nothing to be done about that, unfortunately. Bad water pressure out here.) I was confused. I found myself breathlessly pitching ideas at her for the next book:

'Let's forget about the chick lit this time,' I blabbered. 'How about something serious for once? How about something on the nationalisation of childhood, for example? Or how about something on the citizen as slave? There's bound to be a market in that!'

She looked at me as though I was insane. Which of course I'm not. And asked how the children were faring.

They're faring OK, by the way. Under the circumstances. Actually, since moving to the cottage life has improved significantly for us all. We can eat together now, outside of a bathroom. We can talk endlessly about cows

There are some beautiful Highland calves in the field opposite; an unusually congenial breed, my daughter tells me. So I thought, for lack of alternatives, I might try to befriend them. I thought I could take them a carrot. Do cows eat carrots? I'm sure they do. Are they interested in the nationalisation of childhood? Very possibly.

Which brings me round to the hair again. Or I think it does. The point is, until this morning those little Highlands and I were looking virtually interchangeable, and in a way that was good. It gave us some common ground, I felt … But then finally this morning, I broke.

Ages ago, before all this craziness began, I asked some of the coffee-morning gals where they got their hair done. Only to make conversation, of course, since – famously – getting a haircut in the provinces is the classic Step One in a gal's descent towards eternal frumpiness. It didn't occur to me I would ever take their advice.

But situations change. Don't they just. There comes a time when a person whose cottage smells mostly of cowpats simply has to admit defeat.

So I made the call. Trudi, Deputy Chief Stylist at Hair Today, just behind Market Street, said she was available at once. Trudi, that is, who was charging less than a quarter what my hairdresser charges in

London. She was cheap, and – honestly – she was a human. Someone to talk to. I couldn't resist.

But Trudy wasn't remotely concerned about the nationalisation of childhood. She wasn't even going on bloody holiday. And now, on top of everything else, I look like Bonnie Tyler. I have to wear a hat at the school gate, my daughter insists, and my calf-befriending dreams are in ruins. They took one glimpse at the new yellow mane and they've stayed far away from me ever since.

May 28th

Thought I saw Johnny Depp in Waitrose this morning. Which is odd, because everyone says he's in Hawaii. I only saw his back, in any case, but he was wearing a baseball cap, and he was sauntering up and down the aisles in a deliberately diffident manner, I thought, as if he knew it was only a matter of time before a fan riot broke out. Also – he didn't have a trolley *or* a basket. Which I thought was a bit of a giveaway. He had in his arms:

1 bottle of elderflower cordial

1 bumper pack of Mars Bars

and – I can't remember what else. Anyway, it doesn't matter, because it turned out not to be him. It was just a bloke. Not even a very good looking one, either. He gave me the oddest look as I passed him by. Almost as if he was frightened. Maybe I look madder than I think I do. Or maybe it's the bloody hair. In any case, definitely feeling a bit better than I was. Slightly calmer. Also, haven't been sick for three days.

Finished last edits on the novel this morning and finally sent it off. Book isn't due out until after Christmas. So, apart from the column, I'm now officially out of work. How terrifying is that? Very. Also, clearly, I think I need to interact more with the human race. Actually I'm desperate to interact more with the human race. Which means concentrating more on the journalism and less, at least for a while, on the books. Which means I'm going to have to be brave, after all this time out of the loop, and call up some commissioning editors with article ideas. Trouble is, from the middle of this field, and with only the cowshed for inspiration, I'm finding it very difficult to think of any.

May 30th

Another morning. Another coffee group. Rachel Healthy-Snax has taken me under her wing since the blubbing episode, and though it's a little bit embarrassing and sometimes even a tiny bit claustrophobic, I am extremely grateful, and for that reason I am now officially going to stop referring to her as Rachel Healthy-Snax. Even in my head. Even though I can't remember her real name. Because it turns out there's more to her than fruit'n'veg. In fact, on one subject at least, I think she and her fruit'n'veg league of lady friends may be more than a little unbalanced.

There were five mothers at the Coffee Bean this morning, self included, all talking about kidz'n'vegetables, as per normal; boring ourselves and everyone within earshot into a welcome early grave. Then out of nowhere the subject of Clare Gower came up and a rare shot of energy fizzed through the group. It was extraordinary. I've never heard such vitriol – most especially from Rachel. They hate Clare Gower almost as much as Bin Laden presumably hates Mr Bush. Or something.

Anyway I stuck up for her – or I tried to. I started saying something positive, but Rachel literally shouted me down. 'Oh God. Don't pay any attention to *her*,' she said. (Meaning me.) 'Clare's got her claws right in there!' The other mothers virtually hissed. One of them muttered at me to 'watch out', and with that they all turned away.

Whole thing felt like some kind of medieval witch-hunt, actually. Rachel Healthy-Snax announced that Clare and her husband had first met while Clare was 'touting for custom' at a hotel bar in central London. Which would have been funny, I suppose, if it hadn't been so vicious. In any case there came a point when the whole scene started making me feel a bit depressed. Reminded me too much of being at school so after a while I left them to it. Decided I'd prefer to be alone – which, under current solitudinous circs, is really saying something.

Called Clare when I got back. Don't know why. Felt sorry for her. Wondered if she fancied meeting up for lunch. Somebody – the cleaner, I suppose – told me she'd gone to London for the day.

Haven't seen Clare for ages. Not properly. She always seem to be on her way somewhere else whenever I turn up.

Or perhaps she's decided she doesn't want to be my friend, after all. Could hardly blame her.

Or perhaps she's found out about the column? ...
There's definitely something going on, now I come to
think about it. She hasn't returned the last two calls I've
left for her.

Or maybe it's just that she's busy.

June 1st

Ripley wrote a story about a magic stairway this morning
which his teacher thought was so brilliant she took it to
show the headmaster. He's been wandering around with a
beautiful, secret grin on his chops ever since I picked him
up this afternoon.

And Dora did her maths exam last week and came out,
not just first, but first by miles, with an astonishingly
brilliant, not to say spooky, *97 per cent*. Where did that
come from? She doesn't even like maths. So. Everything
else may be in meltdown, but it seems to be turning the
children into geniuses. Which is nice. Baby number three
will have a hard act to follow, poor little thing.

I was thinking Lettice might be a good name, if it's a
girl.

Half term tomorrow. Fin still away. Money leakage hopeless at the moment, what with the rent and everything,
but it's a funny thing – now that I'm virtually unemployed

I can't seem to stop spending. In any case I'm fed up with the rain. I am fed up with Paradise. The children deserve a treat, and now that we're out of the house I'm not feeling quite so ill any more. Took my credit card to a travel agent in Paradise this morning and booked the three of us on a package deal to Tenerife. I told Fin. I think I secretly hoped he might suggest coming out to join us, at least for part of it. But of course he didn't. Can't. Won't. Whatever. Anyway we're leaving tomorrow night – from Birmingham airport, annoyingly, because there were no other flights left. We'll be gone for a week, so I'll be back in plenty of time to write the next column.

By which time, who knows, it might even have stopped raining.

June 8th

Nope. Still raining.

Lovely week, though. Ripley and Dora had the time of their lives, I think, eating chips and ice cream and building sandcastles and watching the whales. Fin called most nights, said he wished he could have come too and I almost believed him. Almost felt sorry for him, in fact, knowing how much he misses the children. Anyway, Fin's still away, needless to say. And I think the three of us are all a little gloomy to be home again.

COUNTRY MOLE

Sunday Times

➤•◄

All this wholesome country air, those little lambs in
their fields, those birds a-singing in their leafy
trees - and I'm in a filthy mood. Can't seem to shift
it. After a week away in sunny Tenerife I discover
it's still beautiful here in Paradise: it is England
just as it's meant to be.

But as I motor easily this way and that, from lovely,
relatively cheap school to spacious, friendly supermarket and, er, oh yes, home again, I gaze at the
busy mums in their leisure-wear, the Important Dads
en route to the London train, the streams of self-
absorbed pensioners shuffling by in their pastel
anoraks ... There is so much propriety; so little
curiosity, so much contentment ... And I want to
scream. Or strip. Or throw a bomb. I had no idea,
before we left London, that England could be like
this! It is, truly, a foreign country out here.
Chock-a-block with bossy, sensible, law-abiding cit-
izens: pasty-faced men and women who will move your
supermarket trolley if they feel it's inappropriately
positioned; who enjoy nothing more than a slow-moving
queue. Good God, it's a *dreadful* place.

– Oops. Did I say that? Damn. These words slip out. Is there such a thing as severe ante-natal misanthropy? Or is it just that it's raining again?

In any case, there I was this afternoon. In Paradise. In the rain. With no obvious means of escape; and children to pick up in just under three hours. I thought I had better make the best of things.

I had two options, or so it seemed. First, to get a lobotomy. That would certainly have helped. Second, to face down all the shocking negativity. Get out of bed (for example) and try to get involved.

Question was, though, where to begin?

The local paper provided a few clues. I discovered that a pothole had stopped traffic outside a place called Eggbuckland. Perhaps I could drive over and fill it up? Or perhaps I could have headed out to the Paradise Keep Fit Association's Annual Festival of Movement and Dance, due to begin shortly. I could have headed out there and, um, danced ... So.

I didn't do either in the end, of course. Couldn't face it. Drove by the empty Dream House to pick up my post instead. There I found an envelope, addressed To All Local Residents, including me; and inside it a rabble-rousing letter from a campaign group called Oakland! Imagine my excitement. Oakland! is currently looking for nominations to join its Action Panel, which nominations can be submitted by any Oakland! member to the chairman direct.

I sniffed local anger. A call to arms! For a

moment I felt quite inspired. Problem was, since I've never before heard of Oakland!, nor – to my knowledge – ever met an Oakland! member, how was I to set about organising my nomination? And on closer examination, was I absolutely certain I wanted to?

Our Dream House stands, along with a handful of others, above a thin, winding road called Oakland Road (or something similar); which road leads eventually into the local town. A useful road, then. Unsurprisingly, people sometimes tend to drive down it.

Not for much longer, though, if the campaigners of Oakland! have their way. According to my newsletter, they have conducted a survey:

Between 7.30 and 9.00 on May 9th 2006 Oakland!'s Traffic Sub-Committee counted 48 cars passing along our road (as opposed to 44, when they counted fifteen months ago).

Not only that.

'Despite clearly displayed Access Only signs, 14 of those 48 vehicles, 54% of which were single-occupant drivers, then crossed into Archway Lane.'

The Oakland! mob wants £15,000 from the local council to conduct a further survey, so they can prove conclusively that the entire area should be closed off to everyone but them. Problem is, I rather like the sound of traffic. Reminds me of the good old days.

So – I am reduced to surfing the net, then, like all the other lonely nutters out there … Anyone else fed up with all the ruddy decency around here? Anyone? I typed in 'Bossy Britain' at some point. And then 'Bossy Britain: South West'.

And, astonishingly, I hit a seam. I have a meeting! It's an anti-ID card rally, with fellow humans, nothing less, and so far not one of them – over e-mail at least – has mentioned kids or healthy snacks, or even suggested they bring along their anoraks. There is hope in the damp air at last. Little England is almost beautiful again.

June 17th

Just finished a ten-minute conversation with Fin without having a single argument. Amazing. Never worked so hard at anything in my life, and to be fair I don't think he has either. Anyway, he says he's coming home at the end of the week. It will be his first time seeing the cottage. He's arriving early evening on Saturday and leaving after lunch on Sunday. I'm going to put in a call to the babysitter, so we can go out on the tiles together once the children are in bed.

Also – decided to stop being a martyr and start putting a bit of pressure on my useless, fair-weather friends. I'm going to swallow my pride and call them up and bloody well *guilt* them into coming down to see me. I'm fed up with spending so much time on my own.

June 21st

Big bad night, last night. Fin and I had no idea where to go for our night on the tiles. We finally wound up, with only an hour before closing time (partly because we got lost; partly because of the argument; partly because it took ages to get our over-excited children into bed), in a skanky-looking pub on the edge of Paradise, in the middle of what I think is the only housing estate in the town.

Interestingly – *intriguingly* – we almost bumped bonnets with Mr Mega-Bux as we were parking up. His car was stopped directly in front of ours. Fin was staring at him like he'd seen a ghost. He must have spotted the girl before I did – a truly rancid-looking little scrubber, poor thing, climbing out of the Mega-Bux passenger seat. It was pretty obvious what was going on. At least I thought it was. Of course it's possible he was simply dropping the babysitter back, or something similarly dull. But at the time I was convinced he was up to something scandalous. Either way, Fin and I both studiously pretended not to have seen him and he didn't appear to see us either.

Couldn't help feeling for Clare, with her wrinkle-lifting nightcap and her peachy négligé. Also couldn't help being reminded of the slanderous story currently being put · around by the Fruit'n'Veg brigade; that she had first met her husband while she was on the game. I told Fin.

But he didn't laugh. At all. Looked quite angry about it, actually. Maybe he wasn't listening. His mobile had just pinged through a text message, I think, and he was scowling over that. In any case his non-response offended me disproportionately, I see in retrospect. So we entered the pub with him distracted and me already on the point of tears. Within half an hour, what fragile peace there had been between us was in ruins.

Two things came out, amid all the rage and drivel.

Firstly, and for the first time, we gave voice to the possibility that *our move to Paradise had been a mistake.* Well, I gave the voice. I said it. And Fin … didn't disagree. He said we shouldn't give up on it yet; we should 'give the place a chance'; and the five words together, though clearly sensible, sounded to me like nothing but the CLANG of a jail door. How long is A Chance, after all?

Nevertheless. We did agree. To give the place A Chance. Another five years, he suggested … I don't want to think about it too much.

The second thing that came out was that I knew he was having an affair with Hatty. He denied it completely, of course. He denied it very calmly. Actually, I've never known him so cold. He said I was trying to sabotage 'a perfectly simple, enjoyable friendship' out of spite. Because I was jealous and chippy and insecure. I said not. I also said a lot of other things which weren't especially helpful or friendly either. I'm always horrible – mad and horrible – when I'm pregnant. I have to recognise that. But when did he get to be so vicious in return? What's his excuse? Anyway, it doesn't make any difference, really. What does it matter? I've asked him to tell Hatt that he's not going to lodge with her after he returns from the Isle of Man, and he's refused. Or he thinks he's refused.

Obviously, I've not given up.

June 26th

Spent the whole day trying to think of ideas for newspaper articles, and I've come up with nothing. Asked Fin if I could do something on androids, using his film as the peg. He wasn't that keen. But I'm desperate, and he didn't exactly refuse, either. There must be something in it ...

Androids: Do They Really Exist?

Or howzabout:

Androids: Fact from fiction – What are they, and what do they wear?

Not funny. No interest in androids anyway. Maybe I should do something on farms instead. Seeing as I'm stuck here in the country. Farms ... What goes with farms?

Farm noises

Farm fresh

Farm subsidies

Farmhouse Cheddar

Fat farm

I had a farm in Africa

Bugger it. The more I think, the more fatuous I become. But none of my usual commissioners call any more. So I've got to take the initiative. Got to come up with something. Got to.

June 28th

Lovely Alexis. Haven't spoken to her for months. E-mailed her last week, pretty much begging her to come down here and keep me company for a bit. I know she's incredibly busy opening a new shop, so I completely didn't expect her to respond – but she's coming to lunch tomorrow! Love her. Love her, love her. Also, got an e-mail from Rebecca saying she'd take the day off work and come down. Funny how it's always the really old friends (apart from Hatty, of course) who come up trumps in the end. Why did I ever imagine I wanted to make any new ones?

June 30th

Ha! Hatt e-mailed me a photograph this morning, out of the blue, with subject heading 'I'm Not Shagging Your Husband'. It was a picture of a new man. Called Angus. He's a banker, divorced, a bit fat and bald, but not bad looking, I suppose, and apparently he's asked her to move in with him. So– what could I do? Apart from feel like a prize idiot. In any case I bit the bait and immediately called her up.

She sounds incredibly happy. She's apologised for being a stupid cow, though suddenly now I'm not sure if she ever has been, except when she told me to pull myself together – and she already apologised for that. I've apologised too. I feel such an idiot. Obviously. On the other hand, if she'd been a bit less wrapped up in her own life and maybe just a *little* less friendly towards Fin, we might have communicated a little more; I might have known that she's been having it off with a multi-millionaire banker for the past seven months, and none of this would have got so out of hand. She thinks it's my fault. She says I've been chippy, jealous, pregnant, mad, paranoid and generally impossible to talk to for months. Maybe I have. Maybe I have … I also think it's her fault. I think she's been pretentious, egocentric, secretive, insensitive, and an all-round bad and flaky friend. She's been having an affair with the guy since January – a month before she threw Damian out. Why the hell didn't she tell me? She ought to have known I was going to be on her side. One hundred per cent. She could have done anything – except steal my husband or torture my children. I would always have supported her. Isn't that what old friends are for?

But the point is, it doesn't matter whose fault it is any more. We've had it out. We've said our stuff, and she's on the train – right now. For the next two nights she's sleeping on the fold-out children's mattress in our tiny cottage, and then at the weekend she's being joined by the banker Angus, his four children and her three, and all nine of them are checking into a hotel. They're not moving in together yet. It's too soon for the seven children. In any case she's happy, and I am very happy for her. I am happy for me, too. I've missed her.

Called Fin – to apologise. I feel such a bloody idiot. God knows, if I hadn't got the bee in my bonnet about Hatty and him, how different the last few months might have been. How different everything might have been.

Or maybe not. Maybe I would have decided he was copping off with somebody else instead. Maybe the thing with Darrell was going to happen anyway. Maybe I've just been using him and Hatty as an excuse. I don't know. Don't know. Don't know. I feel awful. On the other hand he's away so much, and I may well be chippy, jealous, paranoid, etc., but I'm not completely stupid, and I know he doesn't have to be away quite as much as much as he pretends.

Done nothing much these last few weeks beyond child care and marital squabbling, so God knows what I'm going to write about. Pinning all my hopes on the big ID rally tomorrow. Looking forward to it, actually. Expecting to meet a few engaged people at long last. Maybe – crikey – even make a friend. Hatt says she'll come with me, and she absolutely promises not to giggle.

COUNTRY MOLE

Sunday Times

⇒◆⇐

The husband, sensing domestic meltdown, tore himself
away from his film set for a 14-hour whistle stop with
his family in Paradise. Our children greeted him like
a returning God, and I definitely managed not to look
too sour about that. At least, I did look sour, obviously, but I kept my sour face well out of the way.
Stayed in the bathroom until the first tidal wave of
hero worship had faded and then emerged with a grin
any Stepford Wife would have been proud of.

Didn't last. The children went to bed and within
seconds he and I were yelling at each other, initial-
ly about the exact gestation period of a cow, though
actually that was only the trigger: his ignorance of
– and lack of interest in – cow gestation periods
being indicative, I felt, of how little he knew or
cared about our new lives, spent sharing a wall with
a cowshed.

Anyway he's gone now. Whizzed off back to his
adorable androids (gestation period: over in minutes
apparently, and no associated mood swings). What with
one thing and another I don't suppose he'll be back
in a hurry.

Marital crisis aside, I can't seem to find anything much to complain about. The sun is beaming down, and my weird, pregnancy-induced, werewolf-like smelling senses – the same that have driven us from our dream house into a cripplingly expensive studio-cottage-cum-cowshed – have me reeling with delight at the sweet June air. I can smell honeysuckle and jasmine from three fields away. And I do. Stand and smell the flowers for hours on end. In fact I do very little else.

Also I've got a bit more forthright with friends. Stopped pretending this life of sickly, rural isolation is hilarious, and made it clear that, well, I may possibly be going insane. The good ones have all come through; taken detours out of their disconcertingly busy lives to smell the cows and the flowers with me. *All's well that smells well*, I say to them sagely. Once I've got them here. They tell me I should buck up and organise another book deal. And so I will, as soon as the jasmine season's over.

In the meantime there was the Bossy Britain shindy, arranged in cyberspace several weeks ago, during one of my more desperate attempts to integrate with the locals. We met in a pub, six of us (including one who came with me, doing a good-friend detour). We had joined together, or so we proclaimed, to organise local protests against compulsory ID cards.

The other four were men, of course. And there's something about men with very strong political opinions which makes me worry when they last bothered to change their underpants. This dozy, dirty bunch were angry about ID, as lots of us are. But the point is they were all angry for very slightly different reasons. So while I worried, perhaps excessively, about the onslaught their filthy underpants might potentially have on my sensitive nasal passages, they simply sat there and shouted at each other.

'I think we're all agreed that ID cards are a bad thing,' my friend, usually so effective, occasionally interrupted. 'The question is, what should we do about it?'

Finally, Patchy Red Beard (name forgotten) thumped our little pub table so hard it wobbled, and declared we must immediately sign a pledge forswearing ID cards, regardless of consequences. I asked if there might be other, less personally inconvenient tactics we could try first.

'*You!*' he shouted. (I could smell sweat.) '*You've* obviously only come here for the drink!'

It was a little awkward. But I think, with the exception of my effective friend, the same could have been said for all us. In any case the Meeting of the Lonely Hearts broke up soon afterwards, with exactly nothing achieved. I said, 'I imagine we'll meet again shortly,' and they all looked astonished.

So much for local protest. Dr Reid and his evil colleagues clearly have nothing to fear from this corner of Paradise. Except for the dirty underwear, of course, and I suppose he's used to that.

July 12th

I've e-mailed every friendly commissioning editor at every newspaper and magazine I've ever had any dealings with, letting them know that I'm bubbling over with ideas for them, and suggesting that I come up to London and meet them for lunch. Three of the e-mails bounced back, but beyond that no comeback yet. Lucky really, since I'd have nothing to say to any of them if we did actually meet. I've got one idea so far, and it's so lame I'm not sure I'll ever be able to pitch it with a straight face ... But it occurs to me that a lot of people don't like Christmas pudding. Which begs the question, *Why do we keep on eating it?*

Christmas Pudding, yes or no?

If only it was December. If only someone would e-mail me back. In the meantime I'm reading a good book about Stalin. Wonder if I could do something about – er. Also, farming. There must be something in farming. Tractors. Tractor factor. Ukrainian tractors. I've got a brand new combine harvester and I'll give you the key.

Bollocks.

Hatty and I were coming away from the mad ID meeting, snorting and giggling over general uselessness of said event, and suddenly – there was Darrell. It was another beautiful, warm evening, and he was sitting on his own at one of the wooden tables outside the Red Lion. He was looking at us, smiling slightly, I think. He had a pint of beer in front of him, and opposite, in the empty space, a glass of white wine. So. The laughter died. Or mine did, anyway. I think Hatt's may have continued a little longer. But I froze right there in my tracks. I could feel my face, my chest – my entire big, fat, pregnant body – glowing in awkwardness, shyness and general, horrible confusion.

'Hello my dear,' he said, with that lovely deep West Country burr. With the smile. Like he had his own secret joke going. Which he did, perhaps. In a way. I must have surprised him. We hadn't seen each other since the evening in the woods, all those months ago. He'd telephoned me a couple of times, and for a while, when I was stuck in that bathroom, I got into texting him quite a bit, and he always texted me back, though not always immediately, but then gradually even that petered out. He moved on. And of course so did I.

He looked at my bump, which is small but pretty unmistakable. Or at least it was to him. He looked at my bump long and hard. 'When's that one due, then?' he said softly.

I pretended not to hear. Introduced him to Hatt. Gabbled at her that he was the builder of our beautiful kitchen, and that we'd played tennis a couple of times. I gabbled at him that Hatt and I had just come back from a meeting to protest against ID cards, but they were both of them pretty distracted. Darrell said, 'Aahh. So you're the one who knows all the Hollywood film stars.' And laughed – that amazingly sexy, deep laugh. 'Heard a lot about you,' he said.

Hatt just stared at him. The problem with Hatt is, she's pretty astute. She just stared at him, and said, 'Really?' without any expression.

There was a girl coming out of the pub and heading towards the table. Pretty. Probably ten years younger than me. It was time to move on.

'Anyway,' I said.

'Anyway,' he said. 'Congratulations.'

'Nice to meet you,' Hatty said.

He just nodded. Looked at me. But then the pretty girl was taking her seat, and my view of him was obscured. So I said goodbye to the back of the girl's head and Hatt and I went on our way.

Hatt didn't say anything for a while, and I couldn't think of anything to break the silence either. Eventually, she said, 'He's *very* attractive.'

I said, '*Isn't* he!' And we laughed, very briefly, eyes firmly on the pavement. And after that, thank God, we didn't mention him again.

Hatty woke me up in the middle of the night, unable to sleep on our fold-out children's mattress and convinced that she'd solved the mystery of our strangely familiar-looking babysitter. Hatty reckons she was featured on that TV programme *Wife Swap* a few years ago, and funnily enough I remember exactly the episode Hatt was talking about. The wife was cold and strangely unresponsive, just like the babysitter; and she used to put on suspenders and a geisha kit to welcome her husband home from work every day.

So exciting. Almost better than Johnny Depp.

Makes you wonder, though, what happens to the other reality stars, after they've stopped making prats of themselves on national television. There ought to be a support group for them. Perhaps there already is. Or perhaps I should found one. Call it *After Reality, Reality* – like *After dark, Tia Maria*. Or maybe just *Reality after Reality* … Good God, I feel an article coming on!

I wonder if the babysitter will let me interview her? I'm going to ask.

COUNTRY MOLE

Sunday Times

The West Country tourist season has kicked in. Until now our friendly farmer/landlord, who delivers us fresh eggs, free of charge, almost every day, has been keeping the rent artificially low; out of pity, I think, and a sort of knee-jerk support for all reproducing mammals, livestock or otherwise. Sadly, from mid-July his magnanimity is to stop. Prices for our lovely, odour-free holiday-cowshed will skyrocket to a more market-responsive £475 per week, nearly double what I'm paying at the moment.

He and his wife are feeling the pinch, they say, and they're blaming Gordon Brown. I, however, am blaming our very expensive pedigree dog. She's been wandering their farmyard with a post-operative lampshade on her head, a constant reminder to them both of her owner's Marie-Antoinette-style profligacy. It was the dog, not Gordon Brown, nor even the musical sound of my children yelling at one another on the gravel heap outside their back door, which finally caused the camel to break.

Not long ago he informed me, full of enthusiasm, that our dog could earn us thousands if we 'put her to' (I think it was the expression) one of her own, and sold the resulting litter over the internet. He said he knew of an owner whose pedigree dog, for a fee, would be happy to provide the missing ingredient. Well, at the time I smiled and gasped and pretended to consider the idea. But, honestly, money aside, the prospect of introducing any more juvenile life into our family's current chaos made me want to grab our wretched dog there and then, sellotape heavy stones onto her pedigree paws and throw her in the nearest river. Animal lovers will be relieved to read, however, that I forbore. The children would never have forgiven me.

Instead, I took her to the vet and had her womb attended to. It seemed a bit gross, me waddling in there, my own pregnant belly swaying, ordering an end to all reproductive hope in the poor animal. But I've come to realise there's something fairly gross about keeping a dog in the first place. Don't most dogs make a dash for freedom at the first opportunity? Ours does. She loves nothing better than roaming the open country, sniffing flowers and munching on sheep shit. And yet here she is, forbidden even to breed, asleep from boredom most of the time, and facing a lifetime incarcerated with no chance of parole.

In any case, the farmer was in our kitchen only yesterday, delivering a fresh batch of his delicious though slightly muddy-looking eggs. He was telling me all about his last-but-one summer holiday, and in daundered the post- operative lampshade. The farmer asked if she'd been in a car accident, and I panicked. Only a week ago he and I had been swaying with excitement at the thought of breeding her million-dollar puppies. What could I say? 'Well … *yes*,' I said. 'I mean, in a way. I mean, *no*. What I mean is, we didn't want any accidents! It's my husband's fault anyway. He was absolutely adamant …' The farmer turned a bit chilly after that. Which saved me from a more detailed description of the Loch Tummel Campsite washing facilities, but saved me nothing else. If I can afford to spay an animal whose single offspring might fetch a fortnight's peak-season rent on his holiday cowshed, I am clearly in no need of charity. And how can I argue with that? His wife came round this morning, looking apologetic and bearing a printout of usual rental prices for the time of year. She didn't even glance at the dog.

So. Come end of July, it's back to the reeking Dream House, whose nausea-inducing, just-decorated smell (which nobody else notices) is the only remaining symptom of my pregnancy sickness.

I asked the chemist if there was an odour-nulli-fying-ointment you could dab under your nostrils, like the one they used for corpse inspections in *Silence of the Lambs*. But apparently it doesn't really exist. I'm considering various possibilities now: foremost among them, setting up camp in a tent on the strangely undulating terrace outside our front door. Not especially comfortable, I suspect, with a five and a half month bump. Nevertheless the children are beside themselves with jealousy.

July 16th

Got a call on my mobile from a feature's editor at ███████
I wrote an article for her a couple of years ago, and she
wasn't particularly pleasant to work with: haughty and
unforthcoming, and needlessly frosty – so much so, in
fact, that I didn't even bother to include her in my round
robin touting-for-lunch e-mail the other week (to which,
by the way, I have yet to receive a single response).

I greeted her absurdly warmly, of course. And regretted
it immediately: her frosty tone grew very quickly several
degrees frostier. In fact, I got the distinct impression she
was extremely annoyed to be talking to me at all. Probably
because it was in the back of her mind, as it was in mine,
that the last time we'd had any contact I had e-mailed her
an idea and she hadn't even bothered to acknowledge it.
Snooty cow. Anyway, we brushed deftly over all that. She
obviously wanted something from me now.

I asked after her welfare with the usual arse-licking
concern. And while she replied – at surprising length:
PMT and everything – I was flicking increasingly ferocious
V signs at the children, who were fighting over chocolate
biscuits around my feet. They paid no attention, so I
slipped out of the cottage and locked myself in the car.
The rest of the conversation took place with Ripley and

Dora rolling around in the mud beside my front wheel, punching each other's lights out.

Anyway – that's my excuse. Plus I'm out of practice. Pregnant. Living out in the sticks, and so on. In my enthusiasm to find work I've gone and got myself into a bit of a pickle.

She rang because she'd heard on the grapevine that I was incredibly unhappy living in the country and on the point of moving back to London again. She wondered if I'd like to write a piece explaining why … Slightly disconcerting, it was. Where the hell did she hear that from? In any case, I quickly reassured her, and myself, that the family had never been happier and that there were no plans whatsoever to move back to London. Yet. She sounded quite disappointed.

She said, 'Oh, well – look. If you do get unhappy, this is my direct line. We'd love you to write something for us.' And she was about to hang up – but by then, even with the children ripping hair from each other's scalps in front of me, I had collected myself enough to realise that this was an opportunity not to be missed.

Hold up, Smartypants! I cried (with my internal voice). 'Actually Charlotte – sorry, you're probably in a dreadful rush but would you mind very much – if it's not too irritating – could I quickly give you a few ideas of my own – if you've got a quick minute, perhaps I could …'

Never, I think, in the history of time, has a single, quick minute been bestowed with such filthy, self-important, rotten grace. Nevertheless. I had it. It was mine, and she was listening – more or less.

At which point, I have to admit, the mind went a little blank. The Christmas pudding brainwave went clean out of my head. Also, suddenly, the androids theme felt a bit thin. And any idea even remotely concerning farms or farming has yet to formulate ... Meanwhile old Smartypants on the other end could barely speak, she was so desperate to get off the telephone. It was wreaking havoc on my concentration. So, *in extremis*, and without pausing to think it through, I offered up the only idea I had – and she bought it.

I'm supposed to be filing a 2,000 word interview with the bloody babysitter in six days' time. Assuming the babysitter agrees, of course. Also assuming she really is off *Wife Swap*, which in the cold light of day I realise now she almost certainly isn't. Smartypants was so excited about the suggestion I didn't have the heart to mention that I hadn't actually checked.

She's going to call the article 'Reality after "Reality"', she said.

'Brilliant!' I cried, lickety-spit. Lickety-lickety-lick. 'Charlotte, that's absolute genius!'

To which *she* responded, 'And next time you're in London let's get together and do lunch! I think there's probably loads of country/family-related stuff I'd absolutely love you to do for us.'

So. A turnaround, perhaps. A window of opportunity.

The next step would be to telephone the babysitter, of course. I've been putting it off all day.

Oops. Babysitter not amused. She'd never heard of *Wife Swap*. Didn't know what a geisha was, and apparently didn't have any inclination to find out, either. I think, above all, she was disappointed I wasn't calling to book her for a job, and there's no doubt I could have managed that aspect of the conversation more tactfully. Still, things only turned sour when, in my stupidity and desperation to hear her answer differently, I asked her the same preposterous question again. I asked her *if she was sure*. That she wasn't the geisha off of *Wife Swap*. Why did I do that? Stupid, stupid, stupid. Of course she was sure.

In any case, she didn't like that at all. She accused me of accusing her of being a liar, and I laughed. Which rarely helps. I said, 'Don't be ridiculous,' which again wasn't helpful. 'Of course I'm not suggesting you're a liar. I'm just a bit – well – *desperate*. Ha ha ha.' The laughter sounded totally phony. It sounded awful, actually. I was beginning to hate myself.

There was this glum little pause, during which, I suppose, some tiny, dusty corner of her mind must have been fractionally aroused, because she asked, in her dead-pan, dreary way, 'Desperate for what?'

I tried to explain – about the awfulness of Smartypants, and about how I was trying to resuscitate my journalistic career – and she hung up on me! One minute she was there, the next she was gone. That was it.

So. Anyway. That's that. Disaster. Meanwhile, the search is on for an alternative geisha, I guess. Also, annoyingly, a new babysitter.

Perhaps I should send her a bunch of flowers or something. I think I may have seriously offended her.

July 18th

Finley's androids have finally left the Isle of Man behind. They've set up at film studios just outside London, which means Finley's finally going to spend a bit of time at home, at least at the weekends.

In fact he's taking a day off this Thursday so he can go to Ripley and Dora's Sports Day. So he can knock everyone for six in the Father's Race. Very competitive, Fin is. I'll hardly see him. He's going back to London that night and I'll be away most of the day. But it will be lovely for the children to have him around again; and maybe, after everything – all my stupid paranoia, and everything else which followed – we might even begin to feel a bit like a family again. Maybe.

Also – Great News. Think I've tracked down another interview subject. She lives in Bournemouth and she wasn't on *Wife Swap*, but I don't think it matters. She claims she was on some other reality show about a beauty salon. Also – most importantly – she claims to wear geisha outfits to welcome her partner home from work each night. Or, rather, she agreed that she wore geisha outfits (and numerous other things, too) when I tentatively suggested she might, over the telephone yesterday. She thought it was hilarious, in fact. Lovely woman. So my plan is to go ahead and file an interview with the lovely beauty salon woman, without actually mentioning to Smartypants that anything about her original brief has changed. And if Smartypants turns out to be sufficiently on the ball to notice, which she may be (it's impossible to tell), I'll just have to lie. I'll pretend she misunderstood what I was saying when I pitched her the original idea. I can do that. I think. It's much easier to lie over the telephone. Plus I don't suppose she was listening that closely, anyway. Too busy pilfering freebies out of the Beauty Cupboard at the same time, I should think, if my memory of magazine life is anything to go by. But we mustn't be bitter.

Where was I? There's only one drawback, so far as I can see. I was hoping the new Geisha Wife might have agreed to talk to me just for the fun of it, but in fact she won't do it for less than £250, plus another £400 if Smartypants actually runs the piece. Which means, best-case scenario, I stand to make a minor loss out of the whole operation. But never mind. It's my only commission. The only commission I've had in months, if you don't count the column – and that piece for *Wedding Bells Magazine*, I think it was, or *Big Day* or *Bride & Groom*. God knows. Anyway, I had to do 600 words on White Weddings (Yes or No?). Can't remember which side I took. And I don't think they even ran it in the end.

So. The point is, I'm not giving up on this piece yet. Not giving it up unless I absolutely definitely have to.

Mentioned to Clare Gower & Co that I was leaving Fin with the children for Sports Day (so I could go to

Bournemouth to interview the beauty salon bird). I think they were quite shocked that I wasn't hanging around to humiliate myself in the Mummies' Race. Clare actually frowned – or tried to. Couldn't, of course. She said, 'Mmmvvvv. The kiddies'll be ever so disappointed.'

As it happens, I think Dora is positively relieved. She's embarrassed enough by the fact that I'm pregnant; the humiliation of me pregnant, and puffing and sweating through an egg and spoon race, would probably kill her. So. Anyway, the next day Clare specifically sought me out at the school gate, which she doesn't do often, just so she could invite them all over for lunch. She insisted on it, more or less.

Didn't quite know what to say. Didn't like to accept on Fin's behalf without consulting him first, but the way she put it I felt slightly cornered. She was pretty determined. Prettily determined, I should say. She turned to the children, standing with me at the time, and said, 'You'd like to come to lunch, wouldn't you sweeties, while Mummy's off doing her little thingy?' And of course they would, what with the extra-zingie chocolate muffins, and the ponies and the swimming pool and the trampoline. Not so sure about Fin, though. I told him about it over the telephone last night, and he sounded quite angry.

Never mind – it's only one afternoon. It won't hurt him. Meanwhile I can hardly wait for my journalistic adventure to begin. Even the thought of it makes me feel like a normal, independent woman again.

COUNTRY MOLE

Sunday Times

———◆◆———

Just saw another of those articles about smug, rich, thirty-something metropolitans and their ghastly, healthy 'kids', moving out of London for a life of rural bliss and healthy fulfilment in the West Country. Felt a shiver of shame and revulsion. They used to irritate me enough before, when I believed in them. Or us. Nowadays …

I handed the photographs to my son to draw snot and moustaches on, and considered whether there might be grounds to sue. There ought to be. Because what these meretricious souls always fail to mention, as they parade their family unity inside those big, happy country kitchens, is that life in those kind of kitchens, in those corners of Paradise, does not come cheap. Which means somebody – usually the man in weekend wear at the front of the photograph – has to absent himself from Paradise for long stretches of time, just to scrabble up the money to pay for it. Which long stretches can lead to … Crikey. Where do I begin? More to the point, where will it all end?

But we battle on. My husband and I communicate mostly by text now. He texts sweet messages claiming he's missing us, which I find highly suspicious. I text him to f*** off. At least, now that I check, that was the last text I sent, though I can't honestly remember why. Something to do with my feeling patronised, I imagine, and being left behind in the country to grow old and fat and boring while he continues with life's adventure. That's the usual moan. I have to remind myself sometimes that our situation isn't his fault. No. On the contrary. It's entirely the fault of those New Ruralites, the metropolitans who went before us, who've been posing in their pale green kitchens all this time, acting as if they had found the Answer. I now realise they're all secretly on the cusp of divorce.

Well over half the pupils in my children's school have fathers who spend the week in London. Which means, effectively, and in spite of our marvellous kitchens, our limitless fresh air, proximity to farm shops and so on, the whole 'happy country families' show is nothing more than a sham. I begin to suspect that we none of us converge at all unless there's a lifestyle journalist around to record it.

Oh, I'm exaggerating, of course. I must be. Last weekend I took the dog and the children to the android film set (not on the Isle of Man any longer, but at a studio just outside London) to meet our Primary Breadwinner in person. He was very nice. Nicer than I remembered. We all got on famously, after the initial shyness wore off, and then the dog, the children and I wished him luck with his future money-gathering activities, and took the train back West again. He looked lonely, I thought, as we waved him off.

Back home, we had already left the station platform when I realised our suitcase was still on the train. I yelled and sprinted back, pregnant belly swaying, dog yelping, children squabbling. Two station attendants ran forward to help. One looked after the dog and the children; the other kept the train in the station while I raced through the carriages, desperately trying to remember where we'd sat. It took ages. The process probably knocked out the entire national network timetable (and I'm truly sorry about that). But when I finally emerged with the wretched suitcase, many carriages up, I was faced with nothing but patient, friendly concern. Ten minutes later a woman I'd never met drew up her car and offered us all a lift home …

… And there it was: my epiphany, at the taxi rank. The evening was a beautiful one. Still light and warm, and even at the station there was a lingering smell of summer flowers. I thought of my husband, sweating away in London with his disgusting androids, doggedly continuing with the adventure of life, and it occurred to me (briefly) that perhaps it wasn't me, after all, who was the one being left behind.

July 22nd

Beautiful weather. Amazing what a difference it makes. The children go outside from the moment they wake up until the moment they go to bed. They're down at the stream now, as usual, playing kiss-touch with Mabel and the landlord's mangy sheepdog. I've decided, when we get back to the Dream House, I'm going to invite some friends to stay. I feel so much better I think it's about time we took advantage of this beautiful countryside and our beautiful big house. It's about time we started making ourselves more at home.

Not only that, I think I might even have some of the locals round to dinner. Clare Gower has been so hospitable, it's about time we paid her back.

Anyway, the sun is shining; I have filed my article about the Bournemouth beautician, and I think, in spite of the obvious drawbacks, Smartypants shouldn't be too disappointed with it. Turns out the salon programme's quite famous, so the premise still stands: After Reality, Tia Maria and so on. This time last year she (Tamsyn) was being paid £750 to appear at the opening of a new sex-toy supermarket in Southampton ... When I met up with Tamsyn last week she had just started working behind the bar at a Bournemouth nightclub. So. How have the

mighty fallen. She was a pretty raddled old bird: very mas-
culine, actually, what with the sixty-a-day voice and the
biker uniform. Still, she said she always dressed up for her
partner's homecoming, and it was in both of our interests
to hold onto that. It was the one thing, Tamsyn said, her
voice dripping with emotion, that kept their fifteen-year
relationship alive. If her partner didn't return from work
to find her in stockings and bunny-wear, Tamsyn insisted,
then invariably she'd be in slinky kimono and fishnets …
Unfortunately her other half was away when I visited, but
it didn't matter at all. I left Tamsyn, all togged up in her
geisha gloriousness, blissfully hamming it up for the pho-
tographer. It's going to be good fun, I think.

Suddenly feel full of optimism again. Excited about
moving back into the Dream House. Excited about my
burgeoning journalistic career. Excited about the baby.
Excited about Fin finally being back – if not at home, then
at least in England. Excited about being well again.

Said to Fin if it was a boy maybe we could call it
Ruskin. But he wasn't very interested.

July 24th

… or Ferdinand? Hector? Rory? Kevin? Kevin's nice. Nice
spelling.

Wonder if I should call Smartypants? I filed my copy three days ago now, and she still hasn't got back, lazy cow. I e-mailed her to check she'd received it and she didn't even bother to reply. I'll leave it another couple of days. Don't want to seem pushy.

In the meantime – desperately got to come up with some more ideas …

God it's hot today. Wish I was down by the stream. Perhaps Ripley and Dora might inspire me.

… Playing in streams … the New ?? Something
Farms??
English sheep-dogs
English sheepdogs:
Britain's Cleverest Dogs. Might they be sheepdogs?

Oh, sod it. Maybe I should start packing. Or maybe not. It's too hot. Think I'll go and play kiss-touch with the children.

COUNTRY MOLE

Sunday Times

———◆◆◆———

So we moved back into the Dream House and I've set up camp in the old bathroom again. But I don't think I'll be in here for long. Paradise being what it is, and our Dream House perching as it does (we have to park at the bottom of a fifty-foot hill and climb the rest of the way), there's not much danger of robbers up here. It feels quite safe to leave doors and windows open twenty-four hours a day. What with the fresh air, the box-load of disgusting odour-eating candles kept permanently aflame, and a strict regime of half-hourly toast-burnings, the nauseating smell of not-so-new paint and carpet is finally beginning to fade. I block my nose to cook, and eat alone on our strangely undulating, already dilapidating new terrace – overshadowed now by our neighbour's loathsome poplar saplings. Hatred of both neighbour and her trees has returned with a vengeance, but on the whole it's a relief to be back. The children, especially, are delighted.

I discover that an absolute lack of wear and tear over previous months hasn't prevented our Dream House from sliding into an impressive state of decrepitude.

The new boiler is dead. The garden lights we had installed by the missionary's daughter don't switch on; the new shower in the guest bathroom no longer heats up; the downstairs lavatory is flooding; the guests' lavatory has no water at all; the new carpet has come unglued at the edges, shrunk slightly, and has started fraying. Both doors have fallen off our made-to-measure wardrobe on the landing. The lights have popped in twelve of the fourteen new kitchen cupboards. And our beautiful, expensive kitchen tap has come off its hinges. Which is more of a nuisance than it sounds, since the original designers failed to allow access to the back of the sink without dismantling approx. 60 per cent of the whole kitchen.

– The moral of which woeful litany, obviously, is never to have bought such a big house in the first place, since the more there is of a place, the more there is to be mended. Ownership is a form of Slavery, it turns out. Ah, the hell of being a fat cat.

Months ago, when we first moved in, I took pride in ferreting out the local artisans' lowest prices. Our carpet man, for example (an obvious crook, in retrospect), came in with a quote almost £2,000 below everyone else. And the wardrobe builder wanted £180 for something others said would cost £700–£800. Pay peanuts, you get monkeys, so the old wives have it. Once again, they turn out to be right. Nevertheless when I think of all the cups of tea I made for those monkeys ... and all the thousands of perfectly decent, hard-earned peanuts we handed over, it's difficult not to feel annoyed.

Of all of them, though, the monkey I feel sourest about is the landscape gardener: that same missionary's daughter who first disarmed me with her honest manner, and who then (never mind the floodlights) turned our gently sloping front terrace into a training ground for potential conquerors of Everest. When I dared to grumble about it, her transformation from lovely missionary's daughter to evil maniac was terrifying. It was revelatory.

Nevertheless I would have forgiven her all of that; the shoddy workmanship, my new-found nervousness around the human race – all of it – if it hadn't been for those three unliftable cement sacks she and her lackeys left rotting, and slowly setting, by our front door.

Not that it matters any more. I have a master plan. The children, armed with sharp new tools, are already getting 20p per cupful to tip their chiselled cement pieces over the wall into the tree planter's otherwise immaculate garden. And if that goes unnoticed for a week or so, and the children and I can agree on a price, I'll be sending them over under cover of night, I think, with a tree-felling saw and some strong rope. The children want rollerblades in exchange, but since both are beneath the age of criminal responsibility I think that's a bit steep. The old wives may prove me wrong yet

again, but old habits die hard. I intend to go no
higher than a fiver.

August 1st

Beautiful weather still. Too hot, actually, with my big belly. The climb to the house is becoming more arduous every day. God knows what I'm going to do when I need to get a pram up and down here. I shall have to devise some kind of pulley system or something. Otherwise it's going to be impossible. We shall be trapped up here, pretty much, until the baby learns to walk.

In the meantime I have every window and every door in the house thrown open, and it smells fine. Better than fine, actually. It smells of fresh air and cut grass and roses. And I feel healthier and, excepting my obsession with the Robinson-Horribles and their infuriating trees, saner than I have in many months. Last night I moved out of the bathroom and slept in my own bed for the first time since April. Joy. I'd forgotten how comfortable it was.

August 11th

Back at the Coffee Bean. Once again. Rachel Healthy-Snax and the Healthy Snax league on one table; and Clare

Gower and a couple of the Beauty-Secrets mummies on the other. Hadn't realised until I saw them all in one room quite to what extent the Paradise mummies divided into one or other of the gangs. I suppose, if I belong to either – which I clearly don't – I float between the two. In any case, this morning I so happened to be with Rachel's lot. I went over to say Hi to Clare before sitting down, and she was friendly enough, I think. Perhaps not as friendly as all that. I don't know. But there was a definite bristle in the air as I rejoined Rachel's table.

Any case, a mummy called Jennifer, whom I tend to avoid, broke off, briefly, from telling me about the unusual paleness of the stool which emerged from her daughter's arsehole this morning (despite all the healthy snax) to give me a minor heart attack:

She said, 'Oooh! I bumped into a certain someone yesterday, who says they did a lot of work on your house not so long ago. And they think the world of you! Couldn't stop talking about you, in fact.'

Wondered briefly if my head was going to blow off. I nodded very slowly, without daring to look at her. I said, 'Well. I must say he did a great job. We were both – Fin and I – we were both really pleased with him.'

But she wasn't talking about Darrell. She was talking about the bloody missionary's daughter. Of course. The missionary's daughter had come round to give Jennifer-Mummy a quote for some reterracing, and she was bandying my name as a referee. Amazing. In any case I felt so relieved, or disappointed – or both – I almost burst into tears. Jennifer must have thought I was insane. Assuming, that is, that Jennifer is herself capable of coherent thought. Or of any thought at all. Anyway, I certainly wasn't, at that point. I heard myself gushing about the useless missionary's daughter as if she was not only the greatest gardener in the world but also, possibly, my closest friend. Absolutely didn't enter my head to say anything about the cement sacks. Not that it would have made any difference. Jennifer had already decided to go with somebody else. A Man. She said she wasn't sure why, but that she felt more comfortable having A Man 'doing the garden-y things'. ... *Anyway* ...

Clare Gower and co. left the coffee shop quite soon after we arrived, and there were a lot of stiff smiles and bristly *au revoirs* going back and forth. The Healthy-Snax were whispering about her before she'd even closed the door.

And apparently ... According to Rachel, who heard it from a mother with a son at the senior school, whose husband was having lunch there at the same time, Clare Gower was spotted at the Ivy restaurant in Covent Garden with *one of the fathers from Paradise*. They were having a lovers' tiff, so the story goes, and in the middle of lunch Clare stalked out of the restaurant in tears.

There was a lot of hissing after that. Jennifer said she wouldn't be at all surprised if Clare Gower had AIDS, and that she ought to be forced to wear a sign on her back at all times, warning all and sundry that she was a 'health risk'. Rachel almost wet herself.

I asked how certain they were that it was Clare. I also asked how whoever it was who'd spotted her was so certain that the man she was with was a) her lover, and b) from around here. But nobody seemed to know, and there was a general feeling that I was being irritating for asking. So. Being the heroic sort, I shut up. Truly hate this kind of gang-style bitching. Makes me queasy.

Nevertheless. That's the gossip from Paradise. It's better than nothing, I suppose.

August 12th

Still no word from Smartypants. It's getting ridiculous. She's had the article almost three weeks now. I've e-mailed three times and left messages for her twice. Silly cow. I'll call her Monday. And if she doesn't call me back then I'm going to … do something pretty radical. Not sure what.

Came away from the holiday cottage with a dustbin bag full of nylon camisoles belonging to the farmer's wife, also some jockeys belonging to the farmer. Obviously picked up the wrong sack from their laundry room. Or one of us did, because I think they've got a bag of my pants as well. Very embarrassing. Not sure what to do – except pay a visit to Marks and Sparks, and stuff the bag of farmer's camisoles in a place where, unless he comes hunting for them, I shall never have to think about them again.

COUNTRY MOLE

Sunday Times

———◆———

The secret tree-felling operation had to be aborted in the end. By some terrible fluke, our evil tree-planting neighbours took it upon themselves to be in their immaculate garden one beautiful evening last week, just as my youngest was flinging his cupful of chipped cement over the wall onto their flower bed. It was bad luck. It was also a little embarrassing, because he happened to be standing right beside me at the time of the crime, and if I wasn't quite cheering him on, I wasn't exactly stopping him either. In any case, the incident has put our enemies on their guard.

'Excuse me,' the wife said, with that dreary, modulated, middle-England self-righteousness which tends to make me want to emigrate. – Incidentally I may, at a low point, pre-Dream House evacuation, have suggested that this neighbour-from-hell was in fact a witch who, for reasons I now forget, had cast a sickness spell on me. Now that the sickness and associated hysteria have faded, I suspect that both may, in fact, have been more pregnancy than black-arts related. Nevertheless, it's worth mentioning that the above-mentioned 'Excuse me' came, in all its life-less self-righteousness, from nowhere. She and her voice emerged from thin air, and made us both jump. 'Are you aware that your little boy is throwing bits of rubbish into our garden?' she asked.

I assured her I wasn't, and at once tore a tremendous strip off him. He looked mighty confused, poor lad, but I grabbed him before he could reply, and we both scurried back into the house.

Since then, spurred on by the usual English protectiveness towards castle and garden, the two of them have taken to eating outside every night. Husband and wife – him changed from London commuting suit to the conventional Paradise evening wear of Airtex shirt and high-waist slacks – carry their individual food trays to a small table quite close to our wall, and nibble joylessly on their dinner – *sans* alcohol, I note, and *sans* ever exchanging a single word. It is all gratifyingly depressing.

Of course, if they cut down the poplar trees that are blocking our beautiful view they could let a little more sunlight into their lives, and it would probably cheer them up enormously. But what can I do? They are the authors of their own relentlessly dreary discontent, and I must admit I enjoy watching them slog through it.

I've taken to spying on them from my bedroom window. The children have a set of toy binoculars, with a curious bugging device attached to the top. I would be lying if I said I had never used them. Soon, of course, when their trees grow a little higher, I shan't even be able to do that any longer, and I shall have to return to the old, disheartening campaign of trying to find a friend.

Which campaign, incidentally, though undoubtedly creeping forward, is being seriously impeded not just by own curmudgeonliness, but also by the lack of a respectability-enhancing mate to drag along. I had no idea what a handicap his absence would be.

Country couples, it transpires (perhaps other couples too, but I've never met them before), fear nothing at their social gatherings more than a woman who arrives on her own. Only yesterday I had an invitation for Sunday lunch withdrawn when it became clear that my husband wouldn't be coming with me. Usually, though, things don't even get that far. 'When will your husband be about?' the friendly people inquire. 'We must get you both over to dinner.' To which I quickly reply, 'Sadly he's never around. But I'd love to come.' They answer with embarrassed laughter. I think they think I'm joking.

Either that, or they think I'm trying to steal their gentlemen. Which I suppose I might, a few months down the line, if my own insists on staying away, and if ever I begin to feel human again. But right now, with a slightly disgusting, pregnancy-related spitting problem, and a bump like a balloon under my shirt, it's hard to imagine how I could pose a threat to anyone.

August 17th

Rachel came round in floods of tears, waving a copy of her husband's credit card bill and a matchbox from the Ivy. I tried to be kind to her. Poured her a tumbler of whisky and told her all men were cunts – and I chose the word specifically because I thought it might shock some sense into her. But I don't think she heard me. I could have said anything. She was a total wreck.

'I want to kill her,' she kept saying.

I said something about not leaping to conclusions. That Jeremy eating at the Ivy did not automatically mean Jeremy having an affair with Clare Gower. Lots of people, I pointed out, ate at the Ivy. Hundreds – possibly even a thousand every week.

'Jeremy never eats at the Ivy,' she said illogically, and then disintegrated into tears again. 'It's not his kind of place.'

'There's probably a perfectly simple explanation …'

She's not even asked him for it yet. Or she hadn't this morning. Jeremy was still in London, still blissfully unaware that his cosy little life was in the process of being  smashed into smithereens. Rachel has an appointment with her lawyer first thing tomorrow, and she had a locksmith coming round to the house this afternoon. I tried to persuade her she was being hasty – but I had the wind taken out of my sails a bit, because it turns out this isn't the first time Clare and Jeremy have got it together. It was *Clare* he had the affair with when they first moved down from London. Which explains a lot.

Poor Rachel. Here she was, having surrendered her independence and possibly even her brain, in order to become this perfect, smiling, decent wife and mother – and for what? Her whiney children won't eat vegetables, her husband spends all week away, and the appearance of a single, suspect credit card bill reduces her to this: a vindictive wreck, like some kind of footballer's wife, snarling about alimony and punitive divorce settlements, seething with impotent rage. I think she was terrified. Could I ever become like this? Of course I could. Actually, I ought to be grateful to her. It reminded me to get back to work; to put in a call to Smartypants, to stop coming up with idiotic ideas about sheepdogs and to start thinking about a new book at last. I need money. My own money. I need my own life. I have *got* to get back to work ...

Anyway, I asked her if she wanted me to fetch the children and maybe stay with us tonight, but she looked at me as though I was insane. 'Why would I want to do that?' she said. I had no idea. I didn't really know why she had come to see me at all. Nevertheless, here she was, and in need of support, apparently. After all her kindness to me, which I will never forget, I wanted to help her in any way I could.

I felt a bit silly. 'Why? I don't know. Maybe you and the

children might enjoy the company.' But she said not. Turned out I had misread her completely, once again. She said she'd only come over here *to tell me*. Because she wanted me to know.

'You always sat there looking superior when we talked about Clare Gower. But I was right, wasn't I? That bitch has screwed every husband within a twenty-mile radius of here ... So.' She paused, and then added, spitefully: 'If your husband wasn't already ... doing the business with ...' She had forgotten Hatty's name, and I didn't feel inclined to remind her.

'He's not, actually. I was wrong.'

'Well, I'm just warning you. That's all. No reason your husband's going to be any different.'

She left eventually. I offered to drive her home since she clearly wasn't in a state to do it herself. But her hatred of Clare had apparently contaminated her feelings towards me, too. She shook my hand from her arm as if the contact repulsed her, and she stumbled off down the hill muttering half-hearted thanks for the drink, with the credit card bill and the Ivy matches still clutched tightly in her hand.

I felt a bit shaken up after she left. Called Fin to take my mind off it, and asked if he was the only husband within a twenty-mile radius of Paradise who had yet to have 'done the business' with Clare Gower. He laughed very heartily at that. Said he was in the middle of a meeting. Big surprise. And could he call me back.

Needless to say I'm still waiting.

August 19th

Smartypants answered her telephone by mistake this morning. She sounded very put out when she discovered it was me. She said, 'Oh, hi,' like she'd just trodden in something nasty – almost certainly dog shit. I asked her if she'd read the piece about Tamsyn (which I filed almost a month ago now) and she informed me, with a hint of self-righteousness, that she hadn't had time yet.

'It's been crazy here,' she said. 'Absolutely crazy.'

Nevertheless she promised me she'd 'grab a mo' sometime this morning, and call me without fail before lunch.

Which of course she didn't. So. Called her again at the end of the afternoon, once again taking care to disguise my number, and once again fooling her into picking up. I could hear her inhaling despondently, wretched to discover it wasn't someone more exciting on the other end. 'Oh. Yeah. Hi. I was just about to call you actually,' she lied. 'Yeah. Your article looks … pretty good. From what I've seen. I'll need to look at it again, of course. But I had a flick through. It looks … pretty good. Well done!'

Well done, indeed. I was tempted to test her on it.

So you didn't mind, I asked her, that the piece didn't turn out exactly as I had said it would?

'Mmm? No! Not. At. *All*!' she said adamantly.

I told her we were going on holiday at the end of the week. Suggested that if she needed me to do any changes to the article before that, then she would need to … But suddenly she couldn't wait to get me off the line. Presumably because she'd spotted that the door to the Fashion Cupboard had been left ajar.

So. It occurs to me, suddenly, that she may never actually bother to read the bloody thing. After all my efforts. She may never discover that Tamsyn wasn't quite the pretty suburban housewife we had all hoped for, but an anarchist lesbian aged 73. And a remarkably likeable one at that. In the meantime, perhaps I should quickly send in an invoice. And move on. There are plenty of other features editors in the sea. I've just got to stop being so bloody wet, and telephone them.

COUNTRY MOLE

Sunday Times

———◆———

A freakishly social evening down here in Paradise. First a hearty 'Hog Roast' laid on by one of the school parents as a mid-holiday welcome for our new headmaster, who has at last arrived in the area. And then a dinner party, nothing less. The two combined involved more human interaction than I've had all summer, and more polite conversation than I've endured in a lifetime. But needs must. My cheeks are stiff from so much harmless laughter. My forehead aches with ladylike concern. It was a rotten evening. But who cares? As a result of it, I feel more liberated than I have in years.

Ever since Easter, when news of the appointment first broke, Paradise mothers have been a-frott with excitement at the prospect of the children's new headmaster. Rumours were rife that he was dangerously, outrageously attractive. He looked, according to the few who'd met him, like a younger, taller version of Mel Gibson, and on the strength of that information some women had gone as far afield as Plymouth to kit themselves up with outfits for the evening. If I hadn't been pregnant I might have gone too. Attractive men are in short supply here in Paradise. As, indeed, at least at this early evening Hog Roast, were men of any calibre at all. It was Friday night, you see, and *les mortgages payeurs* were still wending their way home from the battle-fields of London.

It meant Mr Gibson had the territory more or less to himself, and with so many male-starved women to gratify it was impossible to get anywhere near him. I decided to wait my turn (too proud to join the scrum). In the meantime I chatted drearily with two other matrons, both of whom, like me, had husbands who were running late. It emerged they were all on the same train.

Perhaps the train was delayed, we murmured. Perhaps there was a long queue at the taxi rank. In any case (lest anyone start complaining: a big taboo in Paradise) conversation quickly turned to the enormous advantages of our lonely, commuter-wife lifestyles: of easy parking versus congestion charging; of good clean fun and fresh-air-for-the-kids, versus tube bombs and random stabbings; of never having to worry about what to give our absent men for din-dins. Of , er ... I was doing well. On my absolute best behaviour. About to keel over with so much head nodding. About to keel over with boredom, actually, when at last I spotted my husband, pale, drawn and scowling, still on the mobile and writing something in biro on the back of his hand. Knights, it transpires, arrive in many guises. I was never so pleased to see anyone.

Not for long. He was in a terrific temper. The supper we were due to go on to was film-industry related, a work dinner for my husband, and frankly, it's a measure of my desperation that I ever agreed to go along. In any case he'd got the time wrong, and as he arrived to save me from the matrons his dinner host was already on the telephone, berating him for lateness. So we left the Hog Roast squabbling, as usual, and I never did get to meet the Gibson lookalike. I shall have to last out until the beginning of term – which, judging by the glimpse I caught on my way out, shouldn't be too trying. Between the sea of summer frocks, I only saw his slim, blazer-clad shoulders, the point of his pointy nose, his neat and tidy, tiny little head. But it was enough for me to know that he looked nothing like Mel Gibson. He looked like a mildly conceited sports presenter for local TV.

They sat me at the end of the table during dinner, next to another wife. It was after she'd explained to me the pros and cons of biological versus non-biological washing powder and after we'd complimented ourselves on living so close to the fresh air – actually, it was when I heard myself asking for her recipe for birthday cake that I was finally struck with the thought:

This Good Life isn't working.

And there it was, my second epiphany in Paradise: Something Has Got To Change.

August 29th

France. Lovely Alexis and husband have rented a place in the Languedoc. So – an entire week with a house-full of intelligent adults to talk to, and Ripley and Dora reunited with their old friends. Joy. Bliss. Heaven. No need to write the diary at all. We've rented our own place for Week Two. Got Hatt and her very excellent new boyfriend, Angus, and their *seven* children arriving. So. Luckily Hedge Fund Hatt's also bringing a supernanny.

September 3rd

Still in France. Came in from the pool at lunchtime to discover not one, but four messages from Smartypants on my mobile.

Message Number One: 11.45 a.m.

'Ya. Hi. Sounds like you're abroad. Having a fab time. Where are you? Listen – *finally* snatched a mo to have a look at the copy, and I must say the editor *loves* the pics. But I'm a bit confused. Could you call?

Soon As Poss. I'll give you my direct line. Also the mobile. I'm on ...'

Message Number Two: 12.05 p.m.
'Ya. Hi. Don't know if I said it was urgent. Could you call?'

Message Number Three: 12.35 p.m.
'Me again. Where are you? Can you call?'

Message Number Four: 12.45 p.m.
'Ya. Me again. Really need you to call me. Where are you? Could you please call. I think you have my numbers but I'm going to give them to you again ...'

I telephoned her at 1.05 p.m. but she'd obviously already gone out to lunch, and then again at 3.45, but she was obviously still out to lunch. In any case I've not heard a squeak from her since and it's after 7 o'clock now, so I guess she'll have long since waddled off home.

Back to Paradise tomorrow. I'm dreading it. Funny to think – sad to think, actually – almost exactly a year ago we were travelling back from a different part of France, only then we were so full of hope for our future; looking forward to a new life of guilt-free, child-friendly wholesomeness. I was so excited. We all were. This year I've spent most of the holiday formulating secret plans to escape.

Hatt's on my side. She has promised to start scouting out properties for us back in London ... and also, more importantly, without saying anything about it to Fin. She says we were mad ever to have left London in the first place, given how obviously urban we both are. (She might have said so before. Actually, maybe she did. Actually, maybe quite a few people did. Never mind.) She also says we'd be mad to stay away too long given a) the cost of getting back onto the London Property Ladder, b) my obvious unhappiness, c) the impossibility of getting a pram from house to road without two burly men to help me, and d) the dire state of Fin's and my marriage. We don't even fight any more. We just don't speak. I've never known Fin so cold. He won't talk about the future. He won't talk about the baby – let alone the problem of the bloody pram. He won't even discuss babies' names. Ever since – I don't know when exactly – I guess I only really noticed it after I started making an effort myself – after I made up with Hatty – but he seems to be completely wrapped up in his own world. Cold, cold, cold, he is. Sometimes I catch him looking at me …

So. I don't know. Moving back would be such an upheaval, especially for poor Ripley and Dora. They've been through enough this year, what with – everything. Plus I don't suppose I could ever get them back into their lovely London school. And God knows what Fin would say.

On the other hand, he's already so detached. And really, I don't see how things can get any worse between us.

Sometimes I catch him looking at me and I think he hates me.

COUNTRY MOLE

Sunday Times

⟫⋗⋗⋖⟪

Just back from a couple of weeks' holiday in the sunny French countryside. Which was lovely, in a way. Lovely all round. Except as we wended our way home-wards, through pretty French fields and then through pretty English ones, I found myself wondering what the point had been of getting-away-from-it-all, when we started off away-from-it-all in the first place. We live in a rural idyll, for heaven's sake, and Waitrose, with its remarkable Camemberts, etc., is only a short drive away. It would have been cheaper to have invited all our friends to Paradise and stayed put. More importantly, it would have avoided the dreadful, miserable thud of the homecoming.

So, anyway, so much for absence making the heart grow fonder. At the end of our French adventure, sight of the Dream Home did not exactly fill me with glee. Nor did the prospect of the long school term ahead. - It occurs to me, actually, when I picture their cheerful, brittle faces, that my fellow lady-mums are every bit as desperate as I am, possibly even more so, since they don't even have a decent outlet (hello, reader) into which to vent their lonely groans. Over the holiday I've been ruminating about their situation and mine. Mostly mine, of course. I've been forming secret plans.

Which is why, as our journey ended and the car drew up beneath the house, instead of simply bolting, as all my senses swore I should, I stuck around and helped with the unloading. We - husband, daughter, son and dog - scrambled up the long hill to the front door, squabbling about who was carrying what, and how carefully. And then the children slithered quietly away to reunite themselves with the television.

They did not, *nota bene*, slither quietly into the back garden to build dens and pick blackberries; nor into the nearby fields to be reunited with the local fox. Come to that, neither did the husband or I immediately set about exploiting any of the rich advantages of our life here in Paradise. No bracing walk in the fresh country air for us, nor even a tea break to admire the view from our beautiful, undulating terrace. No. He disappeared into his office to talk to a film producer in Bombay. And I, having discovered no chocolate biscuits in the biscuit tin, spent an unsatisfactory half-hour on the internet, skimming through Popbitch.

Meanwhile, yet again, the dog escaped. I'm not especially fond of the dog, as it happens, but, as a fellow Prisoner of Paradise, I'm developing a grudging admiration for her relentless quests for freedom, which is partly why I don't police her as well as I probably should. She has my mobile number on her collar and I get a call at least once a day from a sour-mouthed, disapproving killjoy who has taken it upon themselves to entrap her yet again. Poor thing. I had to rescue her from the dogs' home once. Some officious bastard, presumably wanting to teach her owners a lesson, had dumped her there instead of telephoning. The dog was on the edge of a breakdown by the time I found her, and the wretched home wouldn't release her until I'd written them a cheque for £50.

In any case I was still on Popbitch when who should arrive, huffing and panting at the front door, but the unstable Missionary's Daughter. She was clasping our dog under one beefy arm, seeping with sweat and animal lovers' indignation.

'Alison!' I cried, full of phony friendliness. '*And the dog!*'

'I found her,' she spat, 'all the way down at the garden centre. You're lucky she didn't get run over.' And without another word she dumped the dog at my feet and stomped away.

Alone again, we looked at each other, the animal and I. She seemed cowed and vaguely uncertain and yet, in spite of everything – her hopeless plight, the sure knowledge of the trouble she was in – her docked tail still wagged obstinately on. Something about it reminded me of my lady friends at the school gate …

There is no doubt in my mind any more. Somehow or other, I've got to get out of here.

September 12th

E-mailed Smartypants soon as I got home. Also left her a couple of messages. Nothing. Obviously all the urgency wasn't quite so urgent after all. Called her accounts people and discovered there'd been a payment put through for £150. So. I guess that'll be the kill fee. Never mind. Truth is, what with the baby and everything I'm finding it increasingly hard to concentrate on anything, really. Except escape.

Fin's away again.

Eating breakfast with the children this morning, I happened to mention – *ever so* casually – the possibility of our going back to live in London again.

Dora just laughed. 'You're completely crazy, Mum,' she said. 'I don't know why we even moved here in the first place.' And then, after a pause: 'Does that mean we'll go back to our old school?'

Ripley took it less well. Said he definitely never wanted to live in London again, 'because of the disgusting chicken legs'. Still can't work out what the hell he was talking about, but he did eventually concede that if said chicken leg problem could be overcome he would be more than happy to go home again.

Home.

Oh, I don't know ... Maybe Fin will spend a bit more time with us in Paradise this winter. Maybe, between us, we'll work out a way of getting the baby pram up the garden path. Maybe I'll get used to all this quiet. Maybe I'll find some friends. Maybe I'll be able to forge a career for myself, writing about farming. We've only been here a year and a bit. Even if it does feel like an eternity.

Maybe we should just keep on trying.

COUNTRY MOLE

Sunday Times

———❖———

Vincent, new partner to the old kitchen builder (handsome, non-biscuit-eating etc, etc arrived at last to mend our wobbly tap. I think poor Vincent, though we'd never met before, was disappointed not to find the film producer at home, because Paradise is a small place, and it turns out we all know each other's business. He brought with him a heavy box file filled with his screenplays, and also a film proposal written by his 90-year-old father. It was his father's proposal which seemed to excite him the most. 'It's like *The Da Vinci Code*,' he explained, standing very close to the wobbly tap, but not looking at it. 'I mean, it's like *The Da Vinci Code*. Only more complicated, and also it's better.'

Quite a pitch, I remarked. And one short enough to text.

It was meant to be a joke, but he took the comment  literally; made me text 'LIKE DA VINCI ONLY BETTER' to the Primary Breadwinner there and then. Which I did, partly because, at that stage I would have done anything to get the tap fixed; partly because my husband was in Los Angeles at the time, where it was three in the morning, and texting him with useless information at three in the morning is generally the closest I dare go to checking up on him.

He didn't reply. It tells me nothing, of course. Tells me either he was busy snuffling lines of charlie and shagging some plastic-boobed slapper who wants a part in his next film. Or, erm, he was asleep.

So anyway, less than two months now until the baby's born, and I don't get any more beautiful, or any more fun to be with. It's just over a year since we moved from urban hell to rural Paradise, and let's face it, things haven't exactly gone according to plan. Twelve months ago we were so full of enthusiasm. So full of hope. In retrospect, it all feels faintly embarrassing.

I remember one sunny afternoon in particular, almost exactly a year ago. I took the children into the fields behind the house to pick blackberries, of all ridiculous playing-at-country-life activities. (As if the mangoes at Waitrose wouldn't always taste better.) I remember watching the children shovelling blackberries into their mouths, assuming that this innocent, healthy scenario would be typical of our life to come, and feeling a wave of enormous happiness and pride. My son and daughter had been rescued from a childhood of bomb scares, consumerism and Ken Livingstone-approved street festivals. We were in a field picking blackberries on a weekday. We were doing the right thing. – But then the dog went missing, or my son fell into the stinging nettles. Somehow the spell was broken. And that was it. It's never really been restored.

Which brings me, very nearly, to the point. My husband's last whistle-stop tour in Paradise, before he went off to LA, had been made extra nettlesome not just by my sour face, which I imagine he's growing used to by now, but because I insisted that before he left, all the paintings, plus the twenty-odd packing cases filled with paperback novels I never intend to read again, should finally be brought up from the cellar, where they've been growing mould all winter long.

I'm not sure I ever had much intention of doing anything useful with any of it. But things are so bad-tempered between us now, it's possible I devise fresh new ways to exhaust and infuriate him without my conscious mind even noticing it. In any case the boxes stink of damp. They've taken over the entire sitting room and I can no longer reach the telly. He's been away a week now and I've not gone anywhere near them.

Except yesterday. I bravely put my head round the door. And I looked at the mountain of crap in the middle of our sitting room ... Realised I didn't want any of it ... And then I looked at the pristine, newly painted walls ... And then I did a tour, actually, of the entire house. I wandered from room to unlived-in

room. *What a palace*, I thought. *What a Dream Home*.
I realised, suddenly, that there wasn't much point in
unpacking.

The children don't know it yet. The husband certainly doesn't know it yet.

But between you and me, I've called the estate
agents in.

September 25th

Read somewhere that estate agents have an acronym for people like me, and all the other lonely, house-proud lady-mums with not enough to do and too few adults to talk to: FWOTs, I think they call us. Fucking Wastes of Time. And how right they are ... I sometimes think estate agents may have been invented specifically for us.

Anyway, who knows? Maybe I'm not a FWOT. Maybe, *maybe* I'm doing this for real.

October 4th

Hot. Wretchedly hot. Wish everyone would stop going around in jerseys. Had the windows slightly ajar this morning. So Ripley insisted on eating his Cheerios in bloody mittens. Dora thought it was hilarious and decided to copy him. They giggled and spilt things all the way through breakfast. Very annoying.

October 5th

Darrell came round. The children were at school. The sun was shining. The front door was open, and I was standing on a chair in the kitchen with my skirt tucked into my pants, cooling one of my hot, swollen feet in a sink full of lovely cold water. I don't even want to imagine what I looked like.

I am truly enormous now. *Insortable* enormous, as my posh grandmother used to say. Too bloody monstrously enormous to be seen in public, I think is what she meant. I look like the Michelin man, only hotter. So. Darrell shouted out a hello from the hall before he came in, but the door from hall to kitchen was wide open as well, so he saw me long before I had time to recover myself.

He paused at the awful sight of me, and laughed, and then strolled over to offer me a hand. I leant on his arm as I clambered back down to the ground, and I wish I could say I felt nothing when I touched him. Felt an electric jolt of pure, unrequited pleasure. Like a dirty old man tucking his tenner into a lap-dancer's knickers, I suppose. Christ. What a dismal thought. Anyway. Anyway – never mind all that. Things have moved on since then. Darrell came to see me. And I've often felt that we never really settled things between us properly. I think I felt that in some way I had let him down. So – in spite of my generally monstrous *insortable*-ness I was happy to see him. Very happy.

He made us both some coffee; said he knew his way round the kitchen, which I guess he did. He suggested, with eyes tactfully averted from my horrible swollen feet, that I would probably like to sit down. We took our coffee out onto the terrace, just as we had the last time, all those months ago. And we sat there on the balustrade, just as we had the last time, looking out at the view but not saying much, because I think neither of us really knew quite where to begin. And then of course – inevitably – we both started talking at the same time. He said:

'The old man's in London again.'

It wasn't a question. I wondered vaguely how he knew – except that the old man is always in London, I suppose.

I broke off from whatever I was saying – something facetious but safe about the neighbours' poplar trees, I remember. I nodded. 'The old man's in London,' I said. 'As ever.' I smiled. But I suppose he heard a hint of the bitterness. Or sadness. Or whatever it is. There are times when I can't really hide it.

Darrell nodded. 'Away more and more, is he?' He said it quietly.

'Pretty much.' I stared very hard at the trees; could feel his gaze on my profile; could feel my own eyes burning and willed the tears not to spill over. But then the silence dragged on, and I could sense his – I don't know what: his interest? Concern? Pity? More silence. I looked straight ahead. He looked straight at me. I think I tried to kid myself that he couldn't see that I was crying. He was kind enough not to comment on it, anyway. The silence stretched on and on, and for once in my life I couldn't think of a single upbeat, brittle, smart-arse remark to fill it with. All my energy was focused on trying to suck back those awful tears. Finally he said,

'Well, Martha … Are you going to tell me?' It was the first time, I think, that he had ever called me by my real name. Not 'love', 'sweetheart', 'darling': *Martha*. It sounded shockingly intimate. 'Are you going to tell me or are you going to leave me guessing?'

I – opened my mouth to answer. Hadn't expected the question. Not at all. I smiled, actually, and shook my head. 'No need to guess,' I said. 'It's not yours, Darrell,' And I laughed when I saw the look on his face. He so wanted to believe me, but I could tell that he didn't. 'I promise you,' I said. 'I thought it was yours for a while. I was terrified, actually … Anyway it's not. The maths was out. My maths was out. Thank God.'

He made me promise him again. So I did. Why not? He said he didn't want any nasty surprises. Well, neither do I. The baby's not his. There's no question. In my mind. It never was his, and it never will be, not in my mind. The baby is Fin's – if he wants it. I wish I could believe he did.

After that Darrell put his arms around me and for some reason the electricity I'd always felt before seemed to have ebbed away just a little bit. He might – almost – have been my brother. He was my friend. My only friend, I think, in the whole of Paradise.

I told him we were selling up and moving back to

London; or, rather, that it was what I was planning, but that Fin didn't know about it yet. He didn't seem particularly surprised. He said it was obvious from the start that I wasn't cut out for country life. 'Otherwise,' he said, 'what d'you go so mad with your friend Hatty for?' He laughed. 'You were so jealous of her you couldn't hardly see straight.'

Annoying, that. I wasn't, anyway. I tried to explain to him that it wasn't jealousy. I was *disappointed* because for a while she'd turned out to be such a fair-weather friend. But he wasn't interested. He just laughed at me. Anyway. He stayed for about an hour, I think; until it was time for me to pick up the children. He told me about his little boy Daniel, who started at school this term. He told me about the babysitter's outrage at my suggestion she'd appeared on reality TV. He told me Potato Head had absconded with £4,000 of Darrell's money, and that nobody had heard from him for months. He told me numerous bits of gossip – about people I hadn't even realised he knew. He told me Rachel Healthy-Snax had put her house up for sale. And then, as he stood up to leave, he said:

'I suppose the old man knows, does he?'

'The old man knows nothing,' I said. Didn't really want to talk about the Old Man. Not to Darrell.

Darrell looked unusually awkward. 'Only because … there's a lot of gossip around here. Nasty stories. People round here tend to know each other's business … They can be crueller than you probably think … He's staying away all this time – and you as big as lorry, with the baby due any time now. He may have got the wrong idea. He may be thinking all sorts of funny things … That's all I'm saying.'

I wanted him to be clearer. I think. But he said he had to go. He wished me luck with the baby, and with my secret plans to move us all back to London. It was the warmest of goodbyes. Maybe I hugged him a little tighter than he hugged me. Maybe. But we parted friends.

I watched him saunter back down the hill, out of my life. I'm not sure if I will ever see him again.

COUNTRY MOLE

Sunday Times

———◆◆◆———

The estate agent who showed us the house just over a year ago was utterly wretched when I told him things hadn't worked out for us, and that we were thinking of selling it again. Somehow, though, through the veil of tears, he communicated his willingness to drop by for a valuation. He wanted to come round immediately, even as he was wiping his eyes, but I put him off for a week. It gives me time to smarten the place up a bit; to minimise our inevitable loss-es. I need to get rid of the mountain of musty packing cases still squatting in the sitting room, for example, and buy some lampshades, and put up the roman blinds we had made-to-measure for every room in the house, which have been stacked in the drying cup-board since the week before Christmas, still wrapped in their cellophane …

We spent a lot of money on the back garden, too, when we first arrived. Chopped down a couple of trees, knocked down a wall, built up another. There was a brief moment some time in the early spring, around the time the Dream House stank of chemicals and we all had to evacuate, when our garden in Paradise looked truly stunning. These days, though, it's a bit of a no-go zone: part junk heap, part dog's lavatory. In fact it's probably the most beautifully landscaped dog's lavatory in the world.

We found a giant polystyrene board in the cellar at some point, months ago now, and in an early sign of the slipshoddiness which was soon to take over completely, we used it as part of a complicated barricade, designed to keep the dog from escaping into the village. The system didn't work. Nothing does. Within a week she had gnawed the polystyrene board into a thousand tiny pieces and strewn them all over the garden. Which is where they remain, annoyingly light and bouncy, however hard it rains. What with the dog shit lurking beneath the surface, and all the rest of the junk, we can none of us face the effort of removing them.

But things change. Suddenly clearing up the back garden has become a top priority. As I write, the musical sound of my two children, hard at work in their little rubber gloves, filters reassuringly through my office window. From what I can understand, between their merry screams of disgust, they've so far filled half a dustbin bag with old dog turds and bits of bouncy polystyrene. I'm paying them a fortune, needless to say, though not enough according to my daughter. She claims there's an unwritten rule never to ask an employee to do something you wouldn't be willing to do yourself. Seems pretty illogical to me. In any case - frankly - it's not the only rule I'm breaking this week.

Unless, that is, you're allowed to put a person's Dream House up for sale without quite getting around to telling them about it. Actually the Dream House ownership is split: half the rooms are in my name, half in his. It was a measure advised by our accountants, to minimise the tax bill for our children, should the husband and I simultaneously decide to kill each other. Which we easily might. Or at any rate he might kill me if he knew what I was planning. Happily, at least, there are no tax ramifications in that.

He's away, anyway. As ever. It occurs to me that if I fake his signature on the sale contracts, bribe the children from telling him when he calls, and then somehow arrange to keep our telephone number the same, it could be ages before he even notices we've moved.

Oh, I'm exaggerating, of course. Actually, he's been speeding up and down the motorway to see us often enough recently that he's about to have his licence suspended. But that's not the point. I have to justify my awful behaviour somehow, and since I'm the one doing the writing here, it would be madness not to lay at least most of the blame for this potentially bankrupting experiment on him.

October 14ᵗʰ

Bumped into Rachel Healthy-Snax at the school gate. It's the first time I've seen her since she came round in such a state the other day. Jennifer-Mummy, of stool colour fame, told me Rachel had taken the children to stay with her mother for a while. Anyway, she seemed a lot more composed today. Came over and apologised, in fact.

She said she and Jeremy were getting divorced and that she'd decided, after 'a lot of soul searching', that it was time for her to go back to work. I said *congratulations*. Don't know why. It slipped out. Rachel looked slightly startled, and Jennifer-Mummy, standing beside her as always, pursed her little lips with the utmost disapproval.

'Not congratulations about the divorce,' I said quickly.

Rachel laughed. 'I didn't think so.' She said she was divorcing Jeremy even though it turned out he hadn't rekindled his affair with Clare at all. In fact he had shown her 'documentary evidence' that the person he ate lunch with at the Ivy was in fact a business associate, and not only that, but a man. Rachel seemed oddly unphased by her mistake. She said the fact that she had ever been so suspicious simply confirmed what she had been trying not to accept for a long time: there was no trust between them any longer. 'It's not only that, anyway,' she said. 'The truth is, Jeremy and I have drifted apart. We don't have anything to say to each other any more.'

Afterwards, over more coffee down at the Coffee Bean, Rachel told Jennifer and me how, at the peak of her misery and rage, she had driven over to Clare's house. 'Don't know quite what I was planning to do when I got there,' Rachel said. 'The way I felt, it was lucky I didn't have a gun.'

'*Mmm*,' nodded Jennifer-Bunny. 'Thank goodness for that!'

Clare had answered the front door, according to Rachel, 'looking like the little slut she really is'; dressed in a black silky dressing gown and obviously, from the look of shock on her face, expecting to see someone else entirely.

The confrontation between them didn't last long. Clare had laughed, apparently, and told Rachel *not to be silly*, which must have been a little crushing; possibly the final nail in poor, silly Jeremy's marital coffin. After that, almost immediately, Clare had threatened to call the police. So Rachel left. 'And you know what?' Rachel muttered. Jennifer-Mummy-Bunny and I both leaned forward to find out. 'As I was getting into my car I spotted a *young man* – very nice looking, early thirties – lurking round the side of the house. He was watching me. Waiting for me to leave. I presume she must have told him to park round the back so people couldn't see …'

'There's no stopping her, is there?' muttered Jennifer-Mummy, shaking her fluffy ears. 'It's one man after another with that woman. And I don't suppose *that* young man was the one she was dining with at the Ivy. Knowing the rate she goes ...'

'I wouldn't think so, no,' Rachel said heavily.

'That woman is a Walking Health Risk.'

Maybe. I have to say, the evidence against Clare is slightly stacking up. She's a Goer. No doubt about that. It's no wonder I've seen so little of her. Funnily enough, I was beginning to feel quite offended at the way she seemed to be avoiding me, but clearly she's been rather better occupied elsewhere. Lucky thing.

October 17th

Fin came home this weekend behaving like a different man. He looked happy to be home for the first time in months, I think, as if some dreadful weight had been lifted from his shoulders. I didn't ask what or why – unwilling to rock the boat. It was just lovely to see him like that again.

Also – he turned up with a whole sack of stuff for the new baby: beautiful, ridiculous, tiny little cashmere jerseys, and enormous teddy bears, and a disco-ball mobile to hang above the cot, and booties made of rabbit fur, and a matching rabbit fur hat, and a whole lot of extravagant, glorious nonsense the baby most definitely doesn't need. He said he'd been thinking a lot about names, and what did I think about Ferdinand? Or Hector? Or Rosie? Or Alison?

Alison?

Obviously, not thinking that hard. It didn't matter. It was like having the fantastic Fin I married back home with me at last.

He didn't notice how tidy the house is looking, or if he did he hasn't mentioned it. He didn't ask where all the books had gone either. They've gone to Oxfam. Or most of them have. Two men came up the day before yesterday and spent all morning rifling through the packing cases. They needed a van to take the books away. I spent the afternoon (before Fin came back) carrying their rejects in mini-loads down the garden path to the dustbin. Must have been about forty journeys, and I'm slightly disappointed they didn't bring the baby on. Babies are often born three or so weeks early, aren't they? God, it would be lovely not to be pregnant any more. I can't remember what it feels like to be normal.

Fin says he bumped into Jeremy Healthy-Snax in Soho. He was looking terrible. Like an old man, Fin said. Fin seemed quite shaken up by it. So I updated him on the Healthy-Snax marriage meltdown, Rachel's decision to go back to work and divorce poor Jeremy even though it turned out he'd done nothing wrong.

'She knows he did nothing wrong?' Fin repeated. 'You mean Rachel now knows it wasn't him in the restaurant, and she's still divorcing him?'

That's right, I said.

Fantastic, Fin said.

Fantastic?

Fin just shrugged. Jeremy may be dull, but I thought that was a bit tough.

COUNTRY MOLE

Sunday Times

———◆◆———

Having estate agents round to value one's property can be quite addictive, I discover. They arrive on the doorstep at exactly the time they say they will, wreathed in convivial smiles, bringing with them a guaranteed half-hour not just of adult conversation but of solid, unceasing flattery. Exhilarating stuff. I've just waved the fifth one off. She was still bur-bling about Wow Factors and negotiable percentages as she tottered down the path to her car.

Actually she may have over-egged the omelette a little bit. I don't think we'll be using her. Because there's convivial - and then there's outright obse-quious, and I think she may have crossed the line. She put out a hand as she was leaving and, instead of shaking mine, laid it softly on my enormous belly. 'You'll want to be settled by the time your darling, special little baba arrives,' she said, her mouth all crimped into kiss shape. Crikey. I nearly baba-barfed all over her.

'It's not very likely,' I said to her, politely swatting the hand away. (The baby's due in less than a month.) And then I reminded her - as I've remind-

ed all the agents – not to mention our meeting to anyone. 'It's a small community, and news does tend to
whiz round. Only we haven't quite told the children
that we're moving back to London yet,' I said. 'We
can't quite decide how to break it to them.'

I said 'we' haven't told the children. Obviously
what I meant was 'I', since the husband isn't exactly in the loop yet, either. He's coming back this
weekend and I keep practising different ways to broach
the subject. *'How can we go on like this?'* I'm going
to begin. *'We didn't marry – we didn't have all
these children – only to wind up leading separate
lives!'*

Sound good? God, I hope so. Last time we had a conversation about my misery in Paradise it degenerated very quickly into a disgraceful blubfest. Well, he
didn't blub (though he must have felt like it), I
blubbed for the both of us. It was a few months ago,
and the first time we'd officially acknowledged to each
other that the move from London might have been a
mistake. He suggested we give Paradise another five
years and then maybe think about heading back …

Until that moment it hadn't occurred to me, what
with the Stamp Tax and everything, that escape from
Paradise would ever be possible. I had assumed we
were destined to die here. So I should have been
delighted. And yet somehow the mere mention of actually spending another five years away from London sent
me lickety-spit into meltdown. 'But. I. Just. Hate.
It,' I blubbed. 'I HATE EVERYTHING. I Hate The

251

Walls.' (What walls? I hear you asking. Well, any walls, at that point, but most particularly the ancient, moisture-oozing walls of our next-door neighbour's garden. They obsessed me for a while, along with the trees. Blame the pregnancy.)

In any case, soon those oozing walls will be nothing but a fading memory. Yesterday I called the children's old school in London: amazingly, there are places available for them. Not only that, all the various estate agents seem to agree that if we sell up now we might even be able to cover our losses. Or if not, they're confident we can let the place out. This part of the world is filled with rich London refugees, all of them cash buyers, all of them hovering – sometimes for years on end – waiting to pounce on the perfect place with the perfect Wow Factor. Silly fools.

In the meantime, the market for rentals is booming. So it's going to be fine. I mean it's going to be wonderful. As soon as this baby's born, we're going home.

All I need to do is tell the family.

October 25th

Fin's in New York again and will be for the rest of the week. He promises it'll be his last trip away before the baby is born. But we shall see. In any case it's much better he's not around at the moment. I've arranged to take the children up to London so they can refamiliarise themselves with their old school. It was the school's idea, actually. What a lovely school. Nobody I've spoken to there has laughed at me even once – or at least not to my face, which is all that counts.

When I think of the ridiculous hullabaloo I made at the time the children were leaving – handing over bunches of flowers to the teachers, and possibly even blubbing, and generally being an embarrassing, emotional idiot – I'm actually quite amazed I dared to contact them at all. Even more amazed anyone bothered to call me back. Anyway, they did. Ripley and Dora are nervous and excited. They're going to meet their new form teachers, etc., and then I'm going to spoil them rotten. Force-feed them with Pizza Express, and cinema outings and trips to Madame Tussauds, so that all they associate with the new London is Treats. We're staying with Hatt. Two nights, in fact. Hatt's bought tickets to *Mary Poppins* for the first night.

Obviously I can't ask Ripley and Dora to keep the trip a

secret from Fin. Unfortunately. So – I could try broaching the subject with Fin over the telephone. I could do that. On the other hand I could sort of bank on the fact that children tend to live in the present, and that they will have been home four long days by the time Fin gets back to Paradise. The children may remember to mention the trip, but by then they should have long forgotten the purpose of it.

… Am I completely insane? Am I really going to see this through, and haul us all back to London again? God, I hope so … Or am I simply wasting mine and everybody else's time? I want to believe it's going to happen. I want to believe that I'm not just dreaming. That we're going home. And perhaps, if I say it enough – 'We Are Going Home' –

We Are Going Home.

… It may even come true.

I was rifling around the children's playroom, throwing out broken toys and other bits of plastic, preparing – as ever – for the big move back. Should it come. When it comes … I opened a drawer in the dresser, which I don't think any-one's opened since the week we moved in here. It was unfeasibly tidy. There was a brand new, bumper box of pencils with no tips neatly laid out in there, a bumper box of erasers, a box of sharpeners, several pristine pads of drawing paper, three large, unopened tubs of glitter; an unopened stick of glue; some paper scissors … And the sodding nametags.

God. I remember it, now. All the puerile optimism that went into arranging that stupid little drawer. It was meant to be the Craft Drawer. We were going to be the sort of household which had sticky-back plastic. That was the plan. Sticky-back plastic, and glue, and sew-on nametags. I was going to be like Clare Gower and Rachel Healthy-Snax. I was going to be the sort of mother who spent happy, fulfilled hours on rainy days making useless glittery objects with her children.

Where did that dream go?

October 27th

Column day. Bad day. Bloody bad day to be column day. How the hell am I going to spin this one? Somehow I'm going to have to make it all make sense – with the biggest part of the jigsaw left out. But I'm not writing about it. I'm not. It's absolutely nobody's bloody business but mine. Ours.

Ours, I mean.

Christ, I've been such a fool. I feel such a fool. How could I have been so blind?

COUNTRY MOLE

Sunday Times

———❦———

The husband, looking unusually cheerful, arrived back
from London early last weekend, in perfect time to
pick up the children from school. He said he had good
news. *Ah, extra money*, I thought. (It's all I think
about these days. Have you seen the cost of property
in Shepherds Bush?) I told him that I, too, had some
news which I hoped he would think was good, if not
immediately, then in the long run. But he wasn' t
really listening. He had been approached by a film
company setting up in the West Country, he said. It
might mean he'd be able to spend more time at home.

Traffic, I felt, was moving in the wrong direction.
So I took that moment to inquire about the speed-
camera people, who have been bothering him a lot of
late.

'Any more communications?' I asked casually,
'because I don't see how we can survive out here if
you lose your driver's licence.'

He will lose it, too. We both know that. Sometimes
the gods play into our hands, even when they are
expressly trying not to. I shall be writing a beautifully worded thank-you letter to the magistrates as

soon as their sentence is passed.

Anyway we went together on the school run after that, mostly because I thought it might be our last peaceful half-hour as a quasi-married couple before my good-news-in-the-long-run goes and ruins it all and he calls in the divorce lawyers.

Needless to say, when we got to the school gates he was treated like a soldier returned from the front. (We Paradise ladies do love a man who pays attention to his children.) It was while he was doing his final lap of honour and I was waddling beside him, a monstrously swollen limpet, that we were accosted by a small, fat woman I had never laid eyes on before. I could see the husband wincing as she loomed towards us.

However, by the look in her beady eye it wasn't him she was interested in. 'I hear you're writing all about your experiences in the West Country in one of the newspapers,' she boomed at me. Out of nowhere. Who was this woman? I denied it passionately, of course. 'Ha-ha! *If only!*' I cried. 'Crikey! Imagine all the fun I could have!' But she didn't seem to want to. She said she had also heard on the grapevine that Our. House. Was. For. Sale.

I was still winded from the newspaper bulletin. (Still am, in fact. Is it possible that my secret cover has been blown all this time, that everyone here in Niceland has always known about the column, and they've just been too damn polite to mention it? *Has the joke been on me all along?* What a prospect

- quite a comforting one, now I think about it. Perhaps that's why I've never made any real friends.) In any case, by the time I came to she was already asking about the house price. She said she 'thought' she knew which house was ours and that she wanted to come round for a viewing. My husband was staring at me, I think - I didn't like to check. I stood very, very still and looked straight ahead, as if lost in contemplation.

'Everything all right?' he asked eventually. I said it was, but I must have turned a bit pale because our fat little spy threw a funny into the abyss: something about fetching hot water and towels. Oh, how I laughed. I laughed for ages, until it became embarrassing for all of us.

This, clearly, was one of those deciding moments in life. I could either retreat and deny everything, or I could take full advantage of my temporarily fragile condition and plunge courageously, while people still pretty much had to be kind to me, into the great unknown.

... I shall draw a veil over the private 'conversation' that took place later on that afternoon. Suffice to say, I spent the night on my loathsome in a very nice hotel. The little fat monster is coming for a viewing on Monday. And I am still pregnant and still married. Just.

November 7th

Fin did not want me to go with him on that school run. I realise that now. I climbed into the car beside him, and he was tetchy about it. He looked tense. We didn't talk much on the journey. Then, just as he started the engine his mobile rang, so we swapped places. I drove, and he talked. There was a moment when he signalled at me for a pen and I pointed at the glove compartment. He rifled around, brought out a pen that didn't seem to work; and then there was no paper. He brought a box of matches out of his pocket and started writing numbers with that cramped, untidy handwriting of his. I felt annoyed – but nothing more than that. It was meant to have been a half hour for the two of us, before the children joined in. Instead, it was him and me – and his bloody mobile, yet again. He hung up. I wasn't paying attention to the road, almost drove into the back of a tractor, and because of that we started squabbling. We were still squabbling when we got to the school gates. He suggested I stay in the car to 'rest my feet' while he went out to the playground.

I was tempted, actually. But something – something edgy about his manner made me uneasy. It felt almost as though he was ordering me to stay in the car, and I didn't like that. So I followed him. Clambered out behind him, and then had to struggle a bit to catch up.

Hello Finley! cried all the mothers.

And there was Clare. In her goldy-beige, silk-and-cash-mere twinset. And her stupid brown suede trousers. And her stupid fucking Chanel boots.

She saw him. He gave her a casual wave, I think. But didn't approach. Very impressive. Very cool. *Fantastic* Fin. – No, it was Clare who gave it away. She saw him and me together, me waddling along just behind, and she looked … terrified. She looked just like Mabel does when I catch her mid-shit in the children's playroom.

I thought of her swaying across that stupid sitting room in peachy négligé, *So, Mr Film-Producer* …

I thought of his raucous laughter when I called him up to ask if he was the only man within a twenty-mile radius …

I thought of the way Clare had been avoiding me all this time …

And still, at that point, unbelievably, I didn't know for sure. Until something made me think of the wretched matchbox. Why had it never occurred to me before? Fin goes to the Ivy all the time. Of course he does.

So – I was standing there, watching all the mothers crowd around him. All the mothers, that is, except for Clare. And I shuffled over to stand beside him. Not sure why. I wanted to know if the other mothers knew. *Did they?* It was impossible to tell. I wanted to be sure that Clare stayed as far away from him as possible. And that was when the woman came up to me and asked me about the column. And about selling the house. It was also, I think, the moment when I knew, finally, once and for all and without a shred of doubt, that our little sojourn down here in the Paradise Theme Park was over. Is over. We have to go home.

The children were with us when we got back into the car, of course. I asked Fin if he'd mind showing me the matchbox. That's all. He didn't ask why I wanted to see it, because he knew. He put his hand into his pocket; looked me directly in the eye, and passed the matchbox over.

From the Ivy. Of course. It didn't tell me anything. Of course. Nothing at all. Fin goes to the Ivy all the time.

'I think,' I said, 'we need to talk.'

'Oh, you think that,' he said. And he *laughed*. 'Yes, I think so too.'

We sent the children into the fields behind the house. (How they complained!) And the talking began. And the funny thing is, it was a relief in a way. At least the man that I married – lying, angry cheat that he is – turns out to be still alive. Which is something. At least he has a pulse. At least now, when we talk to each other, we can look at each other again.

In any case. The story.

Fin and Clare saw each other on and off for about a month, maybe two. The 'relationship', if I can call it that, and I suppose I must, started almost immediately after he and I went over to their house for that drink. She called him up about the builder who was mending our kitchen ceiling. Said she was going to be in London. Went to London. It continued from there.

By the time I was driving to Bournemouth to interview

Tamsyn, and Clare was insisting on having Fin and the children for lunch, it had been over for some time. Fin had ended it. Fantastic Fin had come to the conclusion that she was unstable, and that her increasingly hysterical affection for him was endangering his cosy situation at home.

Men are all the bloody same.

On the other hand, I'm hardly one to preach, am I?

Clare found his rejection hard to accept. Impossible to accept. Hence the sobbing at the Ivy.

Hence Fin's irritability at being cajoled into taking the children over to lunch that day.

Hence all sorts of things, of course. His refusal to laugh at rumours about her being a prostitute, apart from anything else. Ha ha.

Her hounding of him, so he says, was just one more reason for him to avoid coming home. Clare was calling him ten times a day. She turned up at his office. Blah blah blah. And then, out of the blue, she rung him up to tell him she'd moved on. She had a new man.

So Fin was off the hook.

But I wasn't.

'... I think you know him,' Fin said. 'Actually we both do. But I think it'd be accurate to say you know him rather better than I do.' I must have looked completely blank. 'Happily, though,' he said, 'Clare tells me that *he* tells *her* that *you* told *him* ... that he wasn't the father. Out by a month, apparently. Is that right?'

Fucking Hell.

COUNTRY MOLE

Sunday Times

Found a place to stay that wasn't too far from the hospital, just in case I went into labour. I ordered room service. Watched telly in bed. It was wonderful. Or it would have been, if certain individuals hadn't been hating me so much. In any case, the husband and I engaged in an extended telephonic row that night which rounded itself off, eventually, in a sort of *faux* peace, because neither of us could face repeating ourselves any longer. The fact is, so I shouted at him (approx. 63 times), if he can't drive, and I can't get the pram up the garden path without the help of a couple of weightlifters, we have no choice but to move. Whether we like it not. And since the children's old school has kindly agreed to take them back again, we might just as well move home to London.

Spent the rest of the night drowning my marital sorrows with KitKats from the minibar, and watching *Relocation, Relocation*, which is always good for a belly laugh.

The small fat mother, who so kindly told my husband that his house was for sale, was standing on our wobbly terrace admiring our Wow Factor view when I arrived home the following morning. She was twenty minutes early for the viewing. It was pretty obvious, though, that she never had any intention of buying. Not just from the beady, furtive look in her eye, but also – how can I put this delicately? Never mind.

In any case, you can never be certain. And it would have been rude and very vulgar to ask. So the husband and I gave her the grand tour. She pointed out a small damp patch in the back bedroom, and wondered aloud if the lavatory in the children's bathroom was leaking. Which of course it is. Then she opened the cupboard on the landing and said 'Ooh,' unapologetically, as the door came off its hinges in her hand. Finally, after chocolate biscuits and coffee, and a volley of questions about why we could possibly be wanting to move back to London, she waddled off, her pretext for hijacking our Saturday morning apparently not worth sustaining any longer.

She was half way down the path when I decided we'd been violated. She had opened the door into our shower cubicle and taken note of our toiletry choices, for Heaven's sake. She had eaten our biscuits, examined our Wellington boots and commented on our leaking lavatory. For nothing. So I shouted after her,

'I take it you're not interested, then?'

She turned back, clearly confused.

'*In the house*,' she made me shout. The husband, annoyingly, was trying to pull me back inside. 'We'll put it on with the agent then,' I called after her. 'Price goes up 1.5 per cent as of this afternoon, ha ha ha! Can't change your mind now!'

She looked at me as though I was slightly balmy, which I thought was a bit rich.

More importantly, perhaps, I had the baby. A ravishing nugget of pure perfection, we all agree, and magically good natured. Goes to show it's a myth, all that stuff about mellow pregnancies leading to mellow babes. Nothing has been mellow these last forty-and-a-quarter weeks. Not even the final ten minutes. The husband and I were arguing about selling versus letting when I finally went into labour. We continued arguing, intermittently, all the way into hospital.

Turned out the midwife's oldest sister used to be friends with Julie Burchill's mother. Amazingly. And so unrushed was the vibe down on Paradise Maternity, and so generous were they with their painkillers, that the midwife and I were able to talk through every detail of Julie's childhood right up until the moment my baby made its entrance into the world. So. A perfect birth.

And a difficult homecoming. We got the baby up the hill eventually. Question is, though, with the husband gone again, I don't see how we're ever going to get back down.

November 13th

Fin's known about Darrell for months, it turns out. My excellent friend Clare told him – and I don't honestly know when or how Clare found out. From what I can make out she knew about the fling between Darrell and me long before she'd even met Darrell. In any case Fin wasn't being especially forthcoming about how he came by the knowledge he had; only that he had it, and that until he got the call from Clare, letting him – and Darrell – off the hook, he had suspected the worst. Or half suspected it, at any rate.

But the baby is his. It is his. So.

I asked him why he'd never confronted me. He said he had every intention of it, when the baby was born. When the 'Clare problem' had been resolved. And when he knew he'd be home for longer than a day and a half, to deal with the fall-out …

It's the thing – aside from the fact he's clever and good looking, and quite glamorous and funny and rich and very good at tennis – it's the thing that made me fall in love with him in the first place. He may be a liar and a cheat – as am I. But he is fair I think; probably the most fair-minded man – person – I've ever met. Which is why he knows, as I do, really, that we are equally responsible for the mess we're now in.

There is no such thing as perfection, and certainly not in a marriage. But I think we can forgive each other. Or something close to it. In fact – honestly – sometimes, secretly, I'm not even sure that there's anything to forgive. I mean, Christ. *It's a long life*. Isn't it? What does it really matter, in the end? In any case I still love him. So. And he and I are going to go home to London with our three beautiful children, and one way or another we are going to stick our marriage back together again.

November 15th

Well, well well. So there I was, lying in bed with perfect Ferdinand, thinking about nothing, for once – not about money, or work, or Fin, or Clare Gower; just lying there being completely, peacefully, freakily contended – and who should call up but Smartypants.

My heart sank, to be honest, because even when she's trying to be friendly she sounds horrible. Anyway, they ran the story. My beautiful, 73-year-old anarchist lesbian, who claims to dress up as a geisha to welcome her girl-friend home, didn't just make the magazine, she made the cover! And the magazine is *out now*. And it's everywhere!

Smartypants said, 'Crikey. Didn't I tell you we were running it? God. Sorree! Totally and utterly thought I had. Are you sure? Fact is, it's just been so crazy round here.

Anyway. Reason I'm calling ...' Turns out Smarty's boss wants me to do more for the magazine. Smarty was ringing to make a date for lunch.

Funny. She sounded thoroughly irritated by the whole affair, even though – presumably – she must indirectly get some credit for having 'discovered' me. Or something. Actually I've been knocking around for years ... Anyway. Who cares? I'm leaving my Ferdinand with Fin and going to London for the day.

Going to interview for an au pair, if I can find one willing to be interviewed.

Going to meet Smartypants at the Coffee Bean. Or equiv. She says she has loads of ideas for me.

Going to be brave and suggest a meeting with the *Sunday Times* people. They must be able to give me a bit more work, especially now that we're moving back to – Oh. Ferdy's awake.

November 20th

Column day. God. It always seems to be column day these days. And I have done nothing. I have thought nothing. I have seen no one but health visitors and letting agents. I have nothing, nothing, nothing to write. About anything. At all.

Health visitors ... Health visitors ... Can I get 700 words out of letting agents and health visitors? Guess I'm going to have to.

Right then. It's going to be crap but I can't help it. My brain isn't working properly quite yet – Ooh, was that Ferdinand?

… Right then.

Right then.

Here goes.

COUNTRY MOLE

Sunday Times

————◆◆◆————

It's like Piccadilly Circus up here in the Dream House. We have letting agents and their weird, whispering tenants filing through the place at least three times a day, and hot on their heels an apparently unending supply of kindly ladies from the National Health Service. They come puffing up that hill one after the other: the tenants with their annoying demands for power showers and fresh licks of paint; the NHS foot-soldiers with their bossy forms and their various bits of measuring equipment, all of them insisting on calling me 'Mummy'.

One of the NHS bods arrived with a machine to test my beautiful, mellow baby's hearing. She asked if Mummy would sign a piece of paper allowing the test results to be released to other government departments. If I refused to sign it, she said sweetly, she wouldn't be able to do the test. The mellow babe could be deaf as a post, and we'd have been none the wiser.

What with the pregnancy hormones and so much time spent in isolation, I've become faintly pathological about a few things: dog germs, for one; the girl in the newspaper shop who takes twenty minutes to serve each customer, for another; the mother at school, who makes her son wear a stupid hat with ear flaps whenever the sun comes out; shop sandwiches; sheep shit … but most of all about Big Brother (the state, not the show). I refused to sign.

Funnily enough, she did the test anyway. So there you have it. Mini protest meets with mini success. The End. I sincerely wish I had something of more interest to report, but I don't. Truth is I've spent most of the last week in bed.

… I have a nasty feeling, mind you, that my mini protest may have landed me on a mini NHS blacklist, because those NHS ladies just keep on pouring through my door. Does everyone get as many as this? Hope not.

I've told them all that we're moving back to London within the next few weeks, and they're absolutely, embarrassingly determined to get a forwarding address out of me. Why? I've told them we don't have one yet but I don't think they believe me, and – intriguingly – in the last few days I've noticed a curious clicking noise every time I pick up the telephone.

NHS eavesdroppers will be disappointed, however, since any plots Mummy may secretly be hatching – to blow up the Home Office, for example – she takes care only ever to discuss over the mobile.

On the landline she and the husband talk about nothing but square footage, room layout and access to public transport. One way or another we are definitely going home.

271

I'm slightly incapacitated at the moment, what with having so many children, and living on a hill that a pram can't get up or down. But the husband has been busy visiting grotesquely expensive rental properties in West London. The plan, inasmuch as we have one, is to get out of Paradise as soon as possible and to be back in London, in a house not too far from the children's old school, in time for the beginning of next term.

What we're looking for, in other words, is a house not entirely dissimilar to the one we sold in Shepherds Bush about eighteen months ago, and which - if we're to believe our former neighbours (all of whom seem incapable of talking about anything else) - has almost doubled in value since.

It doesn't matter, anyway. It'll be just fine. Actually, if we wind up living in a small dustbin it will be all right with me. So long as the pram fits in too. I honestly couldn't care less. Wholesome fantasies about bloody dream homes are a thing of the distant past for me. All I need is a tube station.

December 12th

End of term at last. School carol service.

We had to go, obviously. Clare Gower and her cuckolded Mega-Bux husband sat at the opposite end of the church to us and didn't glance at us once. I wonder if he knows? Afterwards we lingered a little. We had to. I said goodbye to the other coffee mothers. They all dutifully admired little Ferdinand, said they were sorry things hadn't worked out better for us in Paradise, and Fin and I dutifully agreed that, yes indeed, it was a great shame.

But the truth is I couldn't wait to get away. I had no idea, any more, who knew what about either of us, and I felt exposed. I felt like we were the secret butt of everybody else's joke. Or I was. Serves me right, obviously. I know that. But still.

I felt like such a fool.

And maybe Fin did too. I didn't ask.

In any case, we're leaving in less than a week now, and with everything that's happened I'm not certain I can even bear to stick around that long. In fact, as I waved them all fondly goodbye, with that super-rictus Stepford grin chiselled hard into my face, I was praying that I would never set eyes on any of them ever again.

I do not feel proud. Of anything much, right now.

Except the children, of course. But actually I feel much worse about the *Sunday Times* column than I do about any of my other long-running deceptions. And after this week, which will be the final instalment from Paradise, I'm going to say to my boss that the column's got to finish. I'm jacking it in. It's horrible. I wake up in the night sometimes, feeling sickened by my own spite. And maybe I can't help my poisonous outlook, but I guess I could stop sharing it with however many millions of people it is read the *Sunday Times*. So I'll find a more honourable way of earning my living in the future. I really haven't the stomach for it any more.

Coming away from the carol service I felt a sort of camaraderie with Fin that I haven't felt in ages. We all grow older and wiser, I suppose. And even the spoilt ones, like Fin and me, eventually come to understand that nothing in life is perfect. That there is no such thing as a storybook ending.

Frankly, I don't really care what happened in the past, or who screwed who, or when, or why, or what may or may not have come of any of it. We are only human. Or most of us are, anyway. (Jury's still out on Jennifer Bunny.) In the meantime Fin and I will muddle through. Because we have to. Because, in our own messed-up, selfish ways and in spite of everything, or even because of everything – we love each other. And one way or another, I think – I hope – we always will.

COUNTRY MOLE

Sunday Times

———◆◆———

Our letting agents have found not one but two families wanting to move into the Dream House. They've been fighting it out, amazingly, upping each other's offers; hand-delivering cheques hither and thither – and here's the thing.

We've cashed one. We've signed on the line. So it's official. As of Sunday December 17th – in fact as you read this – we'll be double-locking that front door for the very last time. By lunch we'll be gone for good.

What with the packing, and the baby and all, and the husband away again, I thought I could use a bit of help. So I trawled the internet for a temporary nanny, and found Rita. She sounded lovely: gave great text, had a CV with lots of references to her church group on it. More importantly, she could start at once. We arranged to meet for an interview at Paddington Station.

She was significantly older and fatter than I'd imagined. But when I asked her how old, exactly, she looked quite angry and refused to say. We brushed over that. I suppose she could have been anything between fifty and a hundred, say. She had jet-black hair and a totally unlined face.

In any case she had such a warm smile that the subject of mobility, for example, never really came up. I did warn her we lived on a steep hill but I don't think she heard (incredibly noisy, Paddington Station) because she roared with laughter; said she loved nothing better than a hill. At least I thought that was what she said. Might have said she had a son called Bill. She had a strong accent and somebody was having an argument on their mobile at the table next door. The point is, it's not that easy persuading someone to come and work for you when you've got a new baby, and you're moving house, and the house you're moving out of is on a hill and a long way from London, and the house you're moving into hasn't been found yet.

So I offered her the job the moment I suspected she might accept it, and arranged to pick her up from Paradise station the following afternoon. I left her munching happily on blueberry muffins. She looked a picture of health. I'm sure of it.

She made it to Paradise the following day and I greeted her at the platform like a long-lost lover. Dizzy, I was, with the ecstasy of having someone to help. It's probably why I didn't immediately register the limp, and the terrible, horrible panting.

We got her into the Dream House somehow, but it wasn't easy. My son carried her rucksack (mysteriously heavy); my daughter and I (with the baby in a kangaroo pouch) sort of nudged her gently up the pathway. Every three or four steps we would all pause so she could once again re-examine the view.

I think the walk to the house nearly killed her, poor woman. She sat down at the kitchen table and didn't move again until it was time for her to roll upstairs to bed. The following morning she came to breakfast with the rucksack already on her back and without a word of explanation, really – or nothing explicit, and without any direct eye contact Rita, the children and I just clambered back down the hill, into the car and headed back to the station again. We've been sending each other loving text messages ever since.

So – the husband arrives from Budapest on the Friday before we leave. We'll just have to do the packing then. In the meantime I've been rehearsing a Funny for the final moment. As we pull away from Paradise for that very last time, never, ever, ever to return, I'm going to turn to the group, and say: 'Well! That was fun.' See if it raises a laugh.

Unlikely.

I'm not that popular with the family at the moment. But I'll make it up to them. Once we're back in London. With or without poor Rita; with or without a home. It's going to be a glorious Christmas.

Because from now on – and this is a promise – I am going to be a completely different human being.

January 25th
London

London! Thank God. Christmas long gone, and I've not written the diary for weeks. Haven't needed to, that's why. Just haven't needed to.

The children were given an ecstatic welcome back to their old school and they are happy to be home again. Fin is in Utah at the Sundance Film Festival. Doing whatever it is he does out there ... We seem to be getting on OK. Much, much better.

Ferdinand is sleeping. Still the mellowest babe in town.

And I have a new book deal, and a new novel to write and *childcare* – in fact it's astonishing, here we are in late January and I have never felt so positive. Feel fit again. Sane again. Ready for adventure again ...

Also – went to meet my two section heads at the *Sunday Times* earlier today. Turns out I'm not giving up the column after all. In fact, truth is I didn't exactly even get around to suggesting it. Slightly lost the impetus at the vital minute. Everyone was being so nice to me, and then it suddenly occurred to me, it's bloody good *fun* having a secret life. Isn't it?

In any case, over lunch they told me the Editor wanted

to see me. Actually, they said 'John' wanted to see me, and I'm proud to say that I had the presence of mind, on this occasion, not to say 'John who?' So off I tottered, to his very important office. Lots of very important people milling around, looking edgy. I was feeling pretty damn edgy myself.

Turned out he was younger than I'd imagined, though. Not bad looking, either. For a big cheese.

… I wonder if he plays tennis?

HOME

If you've enjoyed...

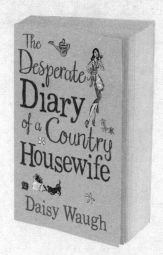

you'll love Daisy Waugh's bestselling novel

Bordeaux Housewives

Read an extract now...

BUSINESS AS USUAL

The family Haunt moved to France for the same reason as most English people. Three years ago they lived in a tiny terraced house in Brixton, South London. Now they live surrounded by sunflowers, in a long, white cottage with pale blue shutters, and they eat fresh oysters every Sunday for lunch. The cottage, aptly named La Grande Forge, is barely half a mile from the small village of Montmaur, where the Haunt children attend school, and a little more than an hour from the beautiful cosmopolitan city of Bordeaux. It stands alone in the wide, flat landscape, pretty as a fairy tale, twinkling with innocence and promise. It has its own vine-covered terrace, its own small orchard of plum trees, even its own small swimming pool.

La Grande Forge was lavishly converted from several ruined barns into one comfortable modern dwelling by the previous owners, who also happened to be English, and whose dream of living the French idyll turned sour at some point, as so many do, for reasons the Haunts assume to have been financial. The region is chock-a-block with courageous, naive English people going slowly broke. Happily the Haunts are not among them. They're not rich by any means but they can afford to continue, for the moment at least. What with

1

everything else, money is one thing they don't much tend to worry about.

Today it is Wednesday. An ordinary, sunny Wednesday in late June at La Grande Forge, southwest France, and Tiffany Haunt and her brother Superman – or *Superrrman*, as the French insist on calling him – are meant to be at school in Montmaur completing their projects on Napoleon. Mr Horatio Haunt (*Père*) is meant to be in the garden digging up organic new potatoes for Montmaur's twice-weekly market, where he sometimes tells friends he has an organic fruit-and-vegetable stall, and Mrs Maude Haunt (*Maman*) is meant to be doing something delightful with the kitchen Roman blinds, which she's been constructing from flat-pack entirely without help for the last two and a half years.

But with the Haunt family there is always a Plan B. As there has to be. Organic vegetables, even when combined with the income from a yet-to-be-realised family *gîte*, are never going to keep shoes on anyone's feet, least of all the French taxman's, whose appetite for shoes, and anything else for that matter, is notoriously insatiable. So Plan B has the Haunt family in a low-key, business-as-usual kind of panic. They have things to do, people to see, and they are lagging behind again.

They also have another Plan for later today, once business is completed, to drive to the coast on a quest for pet jellyfish and a good lunch. Maude and Horatio ($38^1/_2$ each, and both meandering inexorably toward their own personal mid-life crises) believe their strangely clever children know more than enough about Napoleon as it is, and since Tiffany (8) and Superman (5) are already bilingual, better at maths, geography, history and poetry than anyone in either of their classes, it seems to the Haunt parents that they would benefit more from catching jellyfish in the sun, followed by a healthy lunch of *moules à la crème* and profiteroles.

But first Mr and Mrs Haunt have some documents to see to. It's going to take them at least a couple of hours to perfect them and, as always, it is essential no mistakes are made. The documents need to be FedExed to a Rwandan water engineer hiding out in Nuneaton, England, and they have to reach him by noon tomorrow or he and his wife may have to be sent home to Rwanda, where they will possibly be killed, probably be tortured, and where they most certainly do not want to go.

Important work, then, in a small, small, secret way. Not only that, their neighbour and good friend, former Parisian chef Jean Baptiste Mersaud, now Montmaur's favourite builder (and, coincidentally, a strapping man; breathtakingly attractive with that torso, and that dark hair curling at the nape of his neck and those green eyes, and that outrageous *accent français*), has, in desperation, also appealed to them for some small, small, secret help.

The Haunts had never intended to help him, having long ago made it a strict policy to keep the nature of their real work hidden from all neighbours and friends. Apart from which, Maude and Horatio suspect it may be wrong to offer what is, after all, an illegal service to anyone unless they feel them to be in the utmost, deepest and direst need.

But a week ago, last Wednesday evening, when Jean Baptiste came by to fix the kitchen French window he himself had built and installed three years previously, and after he had refused to take payment for it – as he often did – they asked him – as they often did – to stay for supper. Jean Baptiste said yes. He has always liked the Haunts, the air of functional, unsentimental family life which permeates their household. It makes him feel a little less empty, at least for a while. Four years ago, soon after they had moved from Paris back to Montmaur, Jean Baptiste's girlfriend and their two-year-old child were knocked over and killed by a speeding police car.

For a short while the three of them – Jean Baptiste, beautiful Julie, and the curly-haired child – had been a familiar sight in the village square; an outrageously loving threesome; a sight for sore eyes. And now they were gone. He still doesn't talk about them much. He goes about his business as usual, smiling, even laughing, but their absence seems to drip from him. Nobody can look at Jean Baptiste without seeing the suffering.

In any case, it wasn't until after Superman and Tiffany had gone to bed, and the bottle of pineau (a local blend of wine and cognac, lethal but popular) was brought forward, that Jean Baptiste, in his usual mixture of broken, effortful English and very eloquent French, mentioned his other, more worldly, troubles. And he only mentioned them because they were on his mind, and it filled the silence which would otherwise have been filled with his own sadness, which – he was acutely aware – always seemed to bring everyone down. It didn't occur to him that his good friends, the mysteriously unproductive *jardiniers anglais*, might actually be able to help. But, one way or another, and entirely inadvertently, by the end of the evening he had persuaded Horatio and Maude to think the unthinkable... to do the undoable... to jeopardise their entire international operation for the sake of a few French business receipts.

Jean Baptiste is many things – a talented chef and a fine builder, and a keen student of English – but he is disorganised. He works hard, six days a week, long hours a day, and yet barely, in an expensive country and with all the tithes and charges made on him by a bloated government, manages to make enough money to survive. It's a dilemma so common as to be almost tradition among self-employed small French *commerçants*. Like the English migrants who come out to try their luck, they are constantly broke or on the brink of bankruptcy.

Late last Wednesday evening, as the three of them were

4

nearing the end of their bottle of thick and very strong pineau, it became clear that Jean Baptiste was on the brink not only of bankruptcy but of jail. The men from *répression de fraude*, a.k.a. the tax inspectors, were on to him. They were coming on the following Wednesday to inspect his paperwork, the same Wednesday that this story begins.

'*Mais le problème est*,' he said, shrugging his broad builder's shoulders, staring philosophically at the empty pineau glass in his brown builder's hands. They were perched, the three of them, around the large kitchen table; the mended French doors to the terrace pushed wide open, and the soft breeze and the sound of crickets filling the warm evening air. 'My big problem,' he continued, 'it is... *que je n'en ai pas*.'

'*Tu n'en as pas?*' repeated Maude incredulously. 'No paperwork at all?' She frowned at him. He looked green, she thought, beneath the golden brown skin. He looked exhausted. Terrible. '*Mais dis donc, Jean Baptiste. Qu'est-ce que tu vas faire?*'

'*Je ne sais pas*,' he said simply. He shrugged again. He was out of ideas. Out of even trying to have any.

A silence stretched before them. Maude and Horatio glanced at one other, already nervous at what the other might be thinking. They scowled at each other. Shook their heads. Then Horatio stretched across the large kitchen table and carefully refilled Jean Baptiste's glass.

Jean Baptiste looked at it, slugged it back in one, stood up, bumping his head on the kitchen extractor fan behind him as he did so. '*En tous cas* – I am too boring for tonight,' he said, rubbing his head. '*Je m'en vais. C'est la vie, eh?*' He smiled at them both, but it was clear the smile was a strain.

He was on his way out, at the front door and casting a casual, professional eye over a small splinter in the door frame when Maude and Horatio broke. Simultaneously.

'Jean Baptiste. Wait!' they cried. Jean Baptiste turned. 'When did you say he was coming, this *répression* bastard?' demanded Horatio. 'How long have you got?'

'...Because the thing is,' said Maude, '...*C'est possible qu'on peut t'aider, Jean Baptiste* . . . I think we may be able to help.'

Over the weekend, and greatly against their better judgement (if not their better nature), Maude and Horatio knocked up a cargo-load of receipts for Jean Baptiste, and also, while they were at it, various other forms that were missing from his *répression*-pleasing portfolio. Combined, the Haunts' illegal paperwork would place Jean Baptiste Mersaud squarely back on the right side of the law. Which place, considering how hard he works and how much the Monsieur from *répression* gets anyway, is exactly where the Haunts – and Jean Baptiste – believe he belongs.

So. Now the job is almost done. Their work only waits to be delivered. Jean Baptiste has of course been sworn to secrecy; Maude and Horatio have of course refused to accept any payment for their work. And since they are both intelligent, educated people, who believe a moral code is something to be worked out by an individual, not by an avaricious government, or by any government, their major dilemma this morning, as ever in a modern family, is not one of ethics but of time. Tiffany and Superman, the Haunts' beautiful, matching children – round-eyed, round-faced both, with untidy mops of light brown hair and noses freckled by the sun – are impatient to leave for the beach. They want to have a go at catching the jellyfish before lunch.

However:

- it is already ten o'clock.
- the best beach for jellyfish is a forty-five-minute drive from the house.

- the Rwandans hiding out in Nuneaton need their papers dispatched from the FedEx desk in St Clara, eighteen kilometres away, by noon.
- Jean Baptiste Mersaud, who also needs his papers this morning, lives a kilometre or so in the opposite direction.

It seems obvious to most people concerned that, rather than hanging about in their parents' workplace whining about the delay, Tiffany and Superman should try to help out.

'Have you finished the stuff for Jean Baptiste?' Tiffany inquires. 'Is it all ready for him?'

Mr and Mrs Haunt don't reply immediately. In fact, though she's standing directly behind them, and in a very small room with a very low ceiling, they don't even notice she has spoken. So intense is their concentration they may not even have noticed she in the room. They're upstairs, working side by side at one of IKEA's cheapest kitchen tables, in the room they call the COOP (Centre of Operations), which was meant to have been the new baby's bedroom, except Mr and Mrs Haunt haven't got around to having the new baby. They're beavering away on their desktops like the pair of computer whizzos they are, utterly deaf to the world.

'MUUUMMMMMM!' yells Superman, so loud it gusts the papers off their table. They don't respond. Absently, they hold the papers down, and continue working. 'MUUUMM-MMMM! TIFFIE *ASKED* YOU –'

'Forget it, Superman,' Tiffany says calmly. 'This is Jean Baptiste's stuff, I'm sure of it.' From the corner of the messy little room, between light box and the new laminating machine, she picks up a wedge of papers with a yellow Post-It on top, labelled 'J. B. MERSAUD'S STUFF'. She holds it in front of her father so it rubs slightly against the end of his nose.

'Dad? Is this it?'

7

'Yup,' Horatio says, swatting it away. 'Thanks, baby. Can you and Superman drop it off? You know where he lives?'

'Sort of,' Tiffany says.

'*I* know,' Superman says. 'But first I need somebody to help with my puncture. Tiffie, will you help me?'

'He's on the road to Saujon,' Horatio explains, blowing a molecule of dust off his 36-bit flat scanner, reaching for an eyeglass, which he thinks has slipped somewhere behind the machine. 'Head south. It's a bungalow. Not quite

finished. More like a building site. You can't miss it....Anyway, you'll know it when you see it, I'm sure.'

At this exchange Maude is lulled from her highly focused work-trance. '*Heck*,' she exclaims. (Maude always calls Horatio 'Heck'. No one remembers why.) 'Heck, for heaven's sake, we've talked about this. I don't think it's right or fair or *appropriate* that our beautiful, *innocent* children...' She tails off, unwilling to elucidate for fear of Tiffie understanding more than she ought. She shoots a meaningful scowl at her husband, who isn't looking. 'C'mon,' she says. 'We've talked about this. It's out of the question. The children cannot be dragged into all this... any more than they are already. It's wrong.'

'What's wrong?' Horatio asks, all innocence.

'You know perfectly well.'

'Nothing's wrong,' he says brightly. 'Anything wrong, Tiff?'

'Huh? I don't know what you're talking about,' says Tiff, perhaps just a little too quickly. Tiff may be only eight years old, but she's sharp. She doesn't miss a thing.

'*Really?*' Maude turns to her. 'You honestly don't know *why* I should object to you delivering this stuff to Jean Baptiste?'

'Of course not.'

'Do you have any idea what you're delivering?'

'Eh?' says Tiffie. Maude looks at her carefully. Tiffie shrugs. 'Stuff he wants, I expect.' She smiles, as if she's been struck by a new idea. 'Maybe it's stuff he left behind?... Anyway, who cares? Only you said he wanted it before lunch and Superman and me –'

'Superman and I,' Maude corrects her automatically.

'Superman and I *want to go to the sea*.'

It is a source of constant surprise to Maude that her daughter, so intelligent in so many other ways, should continue to be so trenchantly, wantonly ignorant – and incurious – about the true nature of her parents' work. What does she think her parents *do* all day, stuck up here in this tiny room with all this state-of-the-art machinery? Maude smiles at her, half relieved by it, half irritated. 'Well. But even so. Even if you *don't* know –'

'Tiff and her brother have very kindly offered to deliver some stuff to our friend Jean Baptiste. Which he urgently needs, by the way...' Gingerly, Horatio lifts a small PVC sheet from beside the laminator and carries it to the light box in the corner of the room. He has his back to his family. 'I mean, before noon...' he adds vaguely, lifting the retrieved eyeglass, squinting into it. He clicks his tongue. '...S'no bloody good, is it?' he mutters, more to himself than anyone else. '*Bugger*! Maude? Come and take a look at this. Dye-sub's damn well playing up again. It's not bonding.'

'Honestly, Mum,' says Tiff, watching her mother crossing the room to Horatio, bend over the light box, noticing with familiarity the instantaneous switch in her concentration. '...I don't see what you're fussing about,' Tiff continues soothingly. 'We're just giving Jean Baptiste some *bills* or something, aren't we? Because we want to get some jellyfish. I don't even know what... I've no idea... Mum?... Mum?'

'Christ!' mutters Maude. 'That's no good, Heck. It's no good to anyone. Wouldn't get past the people at bloody

Blockbusters. Forget the dye-sub. Don't you think? Go with the Teslin sealer. Teslin should be fine. Hurry up, though,' she adds edgily. 'How much time have we got?'

Horatio turns around while his wife is still tutting over the failed document, signals for Superman and Tiffany to take the package and run. Tiffie winks at him, covers her mouth to stop herself bursting with the excitement of it all. She and Superman carefully, quietly tiptoe over to the open skylight and onto the small, flat, hidden roof beyond.

'Use the door!' Maude calls pointlessly after them as they scamper quickly over the roof pretending not to hear her, scramble down the vine at the far end of the building and leap to the garden below. She clicks her tongue. 'Why can't they ever use the bloody door?'

Bordeaux Housewives

Who hasn't dreamed of running away from it all?

The Haunt family have gone and done it. On an impulse, Maude, her husband Horatio and their two small children have left their tiny London terrace for the sunflower fields and the *vie rustique* of Southern France.

Up the road, the scruffy Hotel Marronnier is about to change hands again. Daffy Fielding has fallen in love with the place and has dragged her husband to France to persuade him to buy it. Which he does – before heading straight back home to his mistress. Can timid Daffy make a life for herself alone?

Watching over all the new arrivals is the glamorous, predatory, eternally bored Lady Emma Rankin. From her exquisite château nearby, she pulls strings to bring the new wives together. But is it Horatio, rather than Maude, who she really wants to sip Sancerre with? Or is her eye on the gorgeous local builder, the only one of them all who is party to the Haunt family's explosive secret?

978-0-00-716820-0 • £7.99

'A witty romp full of joie-de-vivre that'll have you dreaming of summers in France' Closer

Save 10%

WIN AN ECO-FRIENDLY
HOLIDAY AT A UK FARM

courtesy of

Feather Down Farm Days®

Take a trip back to the good old days on an eco-friendly holiday with Feather Down Farms. You could be the winner of a one week stay, for up to six people, at any Feather Down Farm, subject to availability.

Feather Down Farm's unique tented 'cottage' offers an incredible amount of space and comfort in a cosy atmosphere with country style décor from yesteryear and without a computer, TV or minimalist feature in sight! Children will adore their wendy-house style 'canopy' bed whilst adults get to have their own bedroom with a comfortable bed with duvet and sheets. No country abode of yesteryear would be complete without a wood burning stove, oil lamps and candles. There is even a communal oven for baking home made bread and cakes!

Feather Down Farm tents are located on seventeen farms around the UK from Cornwall to Scotland where there are plenty of opportunities for country walks, bike rides and wildlife spotting excursions.

The holiday can be taken before 31 October 2008 or from April to June 2009, excluding all bank holiday weekends, half term and July and August.

Simply log onto
www.harpercollins.co.uk/desperatediary
to enter

For more information on the Farms, please visit www.featherdown.co.uk, or telephone 01420 80804. For full terms and conditions, please see www.harpercollins.co.uk